CHASING FEAR

BY MACKENZIE RICE

ABOUT
MACKENZIE RICE

Mackenzie Rice, Author

LIFE & CAREER

Where do I even begin? How do summarize my life and career into such a small space? It feels entirely implausible, but I will try. My name is Macekenzie Rice. I'm a 30 year old queer disabled woman, semi robotic from multiple surgeries. Lucky to be alive and breathing. I am a Chiari Warrior with Ehlers-Danlos, Mast Cell Activation and POTS. I am a forever college senior, at least that's the running joke. I am a wife and mother to 3 beautiful children. I am lucky.

———————/////———————

I was previously a service advisor and assistant service manager for a Jeep dealership. My world came crashing down in 2020 and I was forced into the worst medical crisis of my life to date. Through fear, obstacles and many of life's curve balls I was forced to pivot my life. After learning I would never be able to drive again I decided to chase after dreams that I had shoved behind closed doors for so long, refusing to let life win.

CONT.

I picked up pen and paper and starting writing, hoping that through words, I could find healing, I could find peace. I found so much more. I found the little girl I had told myself wasn't allowed to chase her dreams, the little girl that wanted so much more in life than to eat, work, sleep and repeat. I am thankful for my journey, thankful for those I have met because of this road, through the many doctors visits, TikTok and other social media sites. I am forever thankful for life's punches and this book is my way of showing the universe that they may take cheap shots, but I am a tough bitch and I refuse to crater, I refuse to cave and I will KO the hell out of anything it throws at me. -Mackenzie

———/////———

RACHEL

A more than deserved mention needs to be made as well. I could not have made it through the last almost 3 years of hell without my beautiful and extremely supportive wife, Rachel. I would not have survived the storm I stepped into back in 2020 without her. She has been my rock, my shoulder to lean on, my ear to listen when I need to rant, vent, scream, cry and blame the world for its cruelty and unfair dispersement of shit. I owe her everything, for standing by my side, for being there without fail, even when things have been undoubtedly rougher than either of us have ever experienced before. I love you Rachel, with all of my heart, with all of my soul and I would cross the world and back just to see you smile. This book, is dedicated to you. Thank you for helping me see my value in the world and for encouraging me to chase my dreams, even when they seem like they are an eternity away. -Mackenzie

CHASING FEAR

SENSUAL LESBIAN THRILLER

DEDICATED TO MY WIFE
BY MACKENZIE RICE

01

CHAPTER

01

My heart beat quickened, my palms began to sweat, the bitter cold air biting at my heels as I ran quickly through the once safe pasture; now dangerous trap. I couldn't escape the fear of what was chasing me. It is and always will be there, staring at me, following right behind, never leaving more than a few inches between us. My eyes still closed, in fear of seeing the monster running behind me, closing in faster, caused me to trip against loose tree limbs on the path. I stumbled but swiftly caught my balance. Refusing to allow myself to fall on the grassy terrain. His icy cold finger tips grazed along my already frostbitten skin; reaching for my sleeve as he lost his grip. I quickened my pace, my lungs burning from the chilly air and continuous running. He is so close I can feel his anger radiating in the air behind me, I can hear his grunts, the groans escaping from the back of his throat. I didn't have time to call the cops, if I stopped for even a second he was going to find me, he was going to kill me.

He is taunting me, letting me use all of my energy. He and I both know he is faster and stronger than I will ever be; the only thing keeping me from stopping is the fear of what he will do. I can't escape the terror he will always leave me with, the stain he is going to leave in my mind, even if I do make it out alive.

I opened my eyes, trying to find a clear path, the enormous trees starting to appear the closer I reached to the woods. I knew that going this way was dangerous, risky, but it's the only chance I had. He could fall just the same as I could. If I kept running in the pasture he was going to catch me, I knew he would.

I continued running, my life hanging in limbo, my legs starting to burn, starting to scream at me, threatening to collapse. I darted in and around tree branches, jumping over logs that had fallen across the moss covered ground, mud splashing up against my skin, covering my clothes.

I looked up and in a split second I saw a stream. I jumped, letting the water fill in around my calves. The water soothing to my burning muscles but soon taken away as he reached for my waist. I tried to pull away, thrashing and flailing my arms and body but his muscles were much stronger than mine. His hand fully grasped hold of me pulling me down, my body flinging in every direction. Unable to gain control as he thrusted me down into the water. Although the water was refreshing to my burning limbs I was being drug down, fully submerged, my already torched lungs about to collapse. The water filled in around my head, my hair swishing in the water as he held me down even further. I struggled and tugged at his body, trying to latch onto anything that would free me from this horrendous monsters grips. I had to get out of his control, I had to find a way to get away from him so I could find help or this was going to be the last thing I ever saw, the last unfortunate place my soul would ever lay.

    I turned my body, flipping as hard as I possibly could, mustering up what minuscule energy I had left. My little arms grabbing his shoulders and pushing as hard as my strength would allow. I raised my knee, shanking and thrusting between his legs, his face instantly turning a bright shade of red and then slowly turning purple. I watched as he fell to his knees, the water from the stream, thrashing all over the both of us. I was freezing but it felt exhilarating, watching him have to suffer like I had.

    He had ripped my jacket off miles back when he first started chasing me, the water only adding to the bitter cold state that my body was in. I turned as quickly as I could, taking advantage of him being on his knees for a moment, trying to gather himself.

    I flung my body out of the stream and kept running, the leaves and trees flashing past my body, the illumination from the moon peaking from behind every corner. I finally stopped for a second to catch my breath and figure out where I was. Turning my head left and right, I was scanning every inch of the forest that I could see, but I had no idea and it was ghostly dark. I had never gone out this far, I had never been in these woods before. I had no clue where I was going or what direction I even needed to be running.

I turned my body towards the direction I had been sprinting from looking and trying to see if I could find him, but he was no where to be found. The trees were all hanging over the sky, making it incredibly hard to make out any of my surroundings. I wasn't sure if he had given up and turned around or if he was lurking behind the shadows somewhere, preying on me, waiting to lurch out in front of me.

He had been toying with me this entire time, letting me get ahead and then catching right back up. My anxiety and fear growing the more tired I became. I wasn't a runner, I never had been, but now that I was faced with running or death, I had no choice.

I pulled my phone out of my pocket, water dripping down the front of the screen from the stream. Fear that it wouldn't work, lying somewhere in the pit of my stomach, haunting me.

I looked all around me again, darkness lurking in every corner, until I found a small spot under a fallen tree branch where I could sit down and hide. There was just enough room for my body to fit under the wreckage of the broken tree, sheltering me from being visible to the naked eye.

I sat down, my legs cramping, my calves on fire. I looked at my phone, dialing 9-1-1 as fast as I could, the service on my phone limited. My phone barely responding to my touches, *the water must have damaged it.* I thought, panic setting further into my chest.

I pressed call and sat there, waiting. The silence becoming deafening, the noises of the woods in the background adding to my stress. I could hear little creaks and cracks of the trees, leaves rustling on the ground, things that sounded like footprints but I had no choice. I had to call the police or I was going to die anyway, I had to get help or it didn't matter how much I ran, he would find me.

"9-1-1, what's your emergency?" A females voice spoke on the other side. Her voice sounded like my saving grace, wrapping a small shred of sanity around me, giving me slight hope.

I was completely out of breath, I was scared to even speak, I knew if he heard me then it was game over, that he would find me and I wouldn't be able to escape his grips again.

"9-1-1, what's your emergency?" The dispatcher repeated, this time, her voice a little more concerned.

"He is chasing me. I don't know who he is. I was walking to my house and saw him lurking on the other side of the road. Before I knew it he was coming for me. I am in the woods on the South side of town, by the "Keller" farm. Please help me. I don't know if he is still chasing me or not, I knocked him down in the stream and then kept running." I said, trying to remember everything I needed to say, all of my words trying to jumble together.

"Okay ma'am, you said you are by the Keller Farm?" The dispatcher asked for clarification.

"Yes, I am." I said, my voice changing to a whisper as I saw a shadow appearing on the tree in front of me.

"He found me!" I screamed, grabbing my phone and standing up, turning toward his body. He was standing there looking at me with a look of sadistic anger, pure hatred. He wasn't just mad, he was infuriated. I tried to make out pieces of his face. Trying to find things about him that stood out but the depth of darkness around us made it impossible to see him.

"Look here, you bitch. This was fun, until it wasn't. I just wanted to toy with you, but now. Now, I just want you dead." He said, his eyes glowing against the moon, the only part of him I could truly make out. I had never seen someone with a look like he had in his eyes, he appeared like all life was gone. It was starting becoming clear why people called murderers stone cold killers.

"Fuck. YOU!" I shouted as I shoved my phone in my pocket, the police still on the line.

I turned as fast as I could and took off sprinting, my legs finally moving a little quicker after my short break. I started ripping tree branches off as I was running and hurling them at him every chance I could. My body refusing to give up; refusing to let him win.

"You can run, but you can't hide Olivia." He said, his laugh echoing in and out of the trees. He had the most horrific and terrifying laugh I had ever heard. It was taunting and intimidating. He stopped to grab a knife from his pocket, letting it snap into place, the sound piercing my ear drums as I realized what he had in his hands. I had been so worried about the knife I didn't stop to realize he knew my name, *HOW DOES HE KNOW MY NAME?*

"You my dear will be the most rewarding." I heard him say, as I darted under a branch, my feet breaking little bits of the earth underneath me. I was very much so regretting wearing vans, my feet slipping and sliding every which direction that stepped, little to no traction on the soles of my shoes.

His fingers grazed the back of my pants, grabbing, his feet sliding just the same as mine. The blade of his knife cutting into my arm, slicing deep, blood starting to drip down my arm. He lost his balance, his feet sliding further than mine.

I kept running, my fears growing the more my arm started to pulsate, my left hand reaching for my right arm, trying to hold pressure so the bleeding would slow down. I could feel myself starting to lose hope, starting to lose faith in my body. I wasn't cut out for this, I wasn't a marathon runner, much less designed for running continuously.

I stopped, out of breath. I didn't want him to catch me but I couldn't keep running, I didn't have anything left in me. I had spent every ounce of energy I had and I was starting to falter. The muscles in my abdomen were starting to feel like someone had twisted them inside out and stretched them apart as far as they could. My calves were starting to cramp up, cramping severely over and over in waves, the pain starting to become unbearable. My throat was on fire, I hadn't had time to think about how I was breathing, fighting for air every second, the cold piercing the back of my throat, making it feel raw.

I dropped to the ground, my body caving out from underneath me, my knees buckling, my head hitting the ground, something sharp stabbing me in the back of the skull. Everything around me started to blur, reality dancing and intertwining with my subconscious mind.

I looked up, knowing, I was done for. I saw him standing over me, his knife still covered in my blood, his eyes beaming and radiating down over the top of me.

"Don't move! Do not hurt her!" I heard a female voice shout, a glimpse of light flashing from behind him. I didn't know who was speaking to him but from the light gleaming in front of her, she looked like an angel.

His menacing laugh echoing around us. "Oh, you going to stop me?" He said, his voice billowing across the wooded area, echoing and haunting, much deeper than it had been before. He turned his body towards the light, his face never completely turning, my eyes unable to make out his facial features. He had short brown hair, his body standard in size. He didn't look like anything special, other than his eyes, his eyes screamed homicidal, crazy even; and he had a tattoo that looked ragged and old. From what I could see it looked like barbed wire peeking from underneath the bottom of the sleeve of his t-shirt.

He looked down at me and callously laughed again, "I'll see you again sometime. Don't think I won't." He said, whispering almost, dropping his body, cowering and running away.

The woman officer took a shot, hitting the tree beside him as he dove the opposite direction, wood blasting across the sky, spraying pieces of bark across the ground as he darted over and under pieces of the forest. She instantly ran towards me, dropping at my body, her eyes seeing the blood dripping from my arm, her hands reaching for my arm, trying to hold pressure, my body going completely limp.

My eyes kept closing even though I was trying to keep them open, I didn't want to be unconscious but it felt like my world was spinning, like the minutes were becoming hours. I felt like I could vomit all over the officer's shoes, my stomach in knots, every muscle in my body shrieking.

The last thing I remember was watching 3 other cops take off running behind us, chasing after him, screaming for him to stop. The lady cop holding my arm, holding the bleeding, her voice hardly audible, "My name is Ivy, I am with the Carlton PD. We will get you help, I promise."

02

CHAPTER

02

"Olivia? Olivia Sanchez?" A voice whispered in a familiar woman's tone. I opened my eyes slowly, trying to figure out where I was, my vision slightly blurry, the room feeling like a twilight zone.

"Yeah?" I answered, looking around the room, realizing I was in a hospital bed. There was a little side table in front of me with a giant water cup, and a plate of food covered with a brown dome top lid. I hadn't even realized it was there. The room was stale and old, typical for a small town hospital. The paint starting to chip around the trim of the walls, the floors scraped and scratched from years of use.

I shifted around in the bed, sitting up slightly, groaning as I realized every bone in my body was sore and throbbing. I looked down, the IV in my hand starting to burn, bruises streaming all up and down my arms, at least the parts I could see. I had a giant bandage from where that asshole had tried to slice my arm off.

I looked over, making eye contact with a woman police officer, her gaze never leaving mine. She was sitting in the recliner beside my bed, a note pad in her hands and a shiny chrome badge on her chest.

"Do you want me to help you sit up?" The officer said, jumping from her chair, sitting the notepad down and walking over to me before I could even respond.

"Yeah, that would be great." I said, my throat burning as I spoke. My voice cracking and faltering with each word I spoke. It felt like I swallowed a glass full of metal shards and they had scratched and torn down the back of my throat.

The officer leaned down beside the bed, looking for the switch to lean it forward, her name tag flashing toward me. *Ivy, that's the police officer that saved me.* I thought to myself as I realized who she was and why she was here, memories from the man chasing me starting to come back in bits and pieces, flashing in and out of my mind, my eyes closing as I realized it wasn't just all a bad dream.

Ivy pressed the button on the side of my hospital bed and let it come forward, my body shifting and leaning with it. The movement from the bed reminding me just how bad my stomach hurt from being chased the night before.

"Thank you." I whispered, my throat still burning. I leaned forward and grabbed the jug of ice water someone had left me, letting the straw touch my lips, the officer grabbing the bottom of it.

"Here, let me help you." Officer Ivy said, her hands holding it for me, her lips pursing to a smile.

"Oh, thank you. Everything hurts, even my throat." I said, handing her the water jug, letting her sit it down on the brown side table in front of me, my arms dropping to the bed. I was physically exhausted, mentally drained and completely unaware of how long I had even been here.

"Yeah, from what I can tell you had a long night last night. Just glad you are safe, you are the first." Ivy said, grabbing her notepad from the chair and sitting back down, her police pants clinging to her muscular legs, her belt buckle shining slightly under the hospital lights.

"What do you mean, I am the first?" I said, turning my body toward her, looking at her for an answer, confused as to what she was talking about.

"I mean, the man that was chasing you last night, we believe he is related to a group of serial killings that have been happening over the last year. Can I ask you a few questions?" Ivy said, flipping the page of her bright blue notebook and letting it fall backwards.

"Yeah, of course… Whatever you need to ask." I said, still trying to digest the fact that she said I might have been, in fact, being chased by a homicidal maniac; a serial killer. That I may or may not be the only person to escape his grips.

"Can you tell me what you remember from last night? Anything at all? There are no details that are too small or unimportant, I promise. I need everything, even before he started chasing you." Ivy said, her pen resting on the paper, her eyes resting on mine.

I laid my head back, taking a deep breath. I really didn't want to remember anything about last night. I didn't want it to even be real life, but here we were anyway living in an absolute nightmare.

"If I need to come back another time, I can…" Officer ivy said, her foot slowly tapping on the floor as the seconds on the clock kept ticking, "I really don't want to overwhelm you. I know what you went through was traumatic. If you need time, that's perfectly okay." She said, starting to close her notepad.

"No… I just need a second." I said, keeping my eyes closed, trying to remember everything, even the beginning of the night, before things changed.

"Okay, take your time. I am in no rush, whatsoever." Ivy said, sitting forward in the chair, opening her notebook up again, the leather part of the chair making a squeaking noise as she shifted her body around.

My mind instantly shot back to the sound of her clanking. Flashing back to the sound of the ringing bells from the local bar as the front door was opening, a slight mist from the rain hitting glass door as it opened.

"I had been out with my friends, we were all drinking and celebrating one of our best friends, Kaley, leaving for the Air Force next weekend. I was sitting on a barstool, my legs crossed against one another, and my arm resting on the wooden bar, my friends were all standing around me when I made eye contact with a man across the room as he walked through the front door. He had short brown hair that was styled similar to a drop fade. He was slightly taller than I am normal-sh build, muscular. He did look road hard and put away wet though. I honestly tried to avoid him most of the night, he gave me the creeps." I said, shifting in the bed, trying to remember everything I could.

"And was that the same man that was chasing you?" Ivy said.

"I think so. But I'm not sure. They had similar body structure, a similar look. But the man who chased me wasn't wearing the same leather jacket that the guy from the bar was. The man chasing me was wearing a hoodie but I never could make out his face." I whispered. The night was still foggy, details still seemingly unclear.

"Do you have any idea how old you think the guy from the bar was? Just a guess even…" Ivy asked, writing notes down in her pad frantically.

"I don't know, I wish I did, but its hard to say. He looked older, well older than me. I was super out of it to be honest, most of the night is extremely foggy. I just don't want to give you the wrong description, that's all." I said, wishing I had gotten a better look at him, that I had taken the time to really pay attention to what he looked like and that I hadn't been pounding down drinks hand over fist. I knew better.

"I had been drinking for hours before he showed up. I really don't even know how much alcohol I had consumed by this point, but it was a lot. He just gave me weird vibes. I kept catching him staring at me from across the bar, my eyes trying not to make contact with his. I didn't want him to know I knew he was staring at me, but I could feel it, his eyes burning into me from across the room. I didn't notice him staring at anyone else, but like I said, by that point I was drunk. I think he might have had a girl with him, or a girl he knew, she seemed to keep finding her way back over by him, but I couldn't ever see her face, she had her back turned to me almost the entire night." I said, shifting in the bed again, trying to find a spot that was even remotely comfortable, my tailbone feeling like it could rupture at any moment. When I had fallen to the ground, my body giving up, I had landed immediately on my tailbone. The pressure from my fall making my entire lower back feel like it could explode, a tree limb piercing my back at the same time.

"Anyway, I ended up leaving the bar as it was getting ready to close. A few of my friends were in tow and we walked home. There was no way I could drive after everything I had consumed and my friends weren't any better than I was. One by one we walked until most of my friends had made it to their houses. I think it was close to 1:30 by this point, but I really can't say that for sure." I said, officer Ivy writing a few notes down and then looking back at me. I stopped and looked at her, her hair pulled back into a ponytail, her beautiful copper red hair perfectly placed. She was jotting down notes, frantically trying to make sure she got as many details on the paper as she could.

"We walked to my friend Sophie's house, she was the last stop before mine. I walked her up to her door, making sure she made it into her house, she was pretty hammered, to be honest. I remember she tried to kiss me she was so drunk. She kept trying to beg me to stay, to sleep on her couch or in her bed..." I said, my face getting a little red, forgetting what all had happened until the words were leaving my mouth. Sophie hadn't ever given me the impression that she was gay or even remotely into women but she knew I was. Maybe that's why she had tried to kiss me, I really had no idea..

Maybe it was because she and her boyfriend had just broken up and she was drunk and lonely, who knows. Regardless, it was weird, we had been friends since we were in kindergarten, growing up together. Living pretty close to each other, almost neighbors.

She was the first friend I had told when I had my period. The first friend that knew when my parents were threatening to get a divorce. She had been there through everything with me, thick and thin. Hell, I had even seen her naked when we had been drunk skinny dipping in high school. I just never had seen her like that, never thought of her as more than a friend, a best friend. And she had given me no reason up until last night to believe she wanted more either.

"I didn't want to do anything stupid or ruin our friendship. I just don't see her that way, so I made sure she was in bed safe and sound and then I left. She kept telling me not to leave that she was worried about that weird guy from the bar but I told her not to worry; that I hadn't seen him since we had left and she was just drunk and paranoid…" I whispered, realizing that she had tried to warn me. She had tried to stop me so I wouldn't be walking alone, but I, being drunk, had decided I was just fine.

"I stopped in her kitchen and got a glass of water before I left, trying to sober up as best as I could. By this point, I wasn't near as drunk as I had been when I left the bar, but I could still feel the alcohol. I walked out of her house, locking the front door with my spare key and then stepped down her front porch steps. I remember turning back to make sure that I had shut her storm door behind me. And that's when I saw him in the reflection of the glass…" I said, pain striking my chest, a sharp stabbing jolt of electricity overcoming my body.

"Take your time. Don't rush through it. You are doing perfect Olivia." Ivy said, standing up and walking over towards the bed. "Just close your eyes, this is the part I need the most. I need you to remember whatever you can, as much as you can." Ivy said, her pen sitting on the paper under her hands, waiting to get as much information as she could.

  I took a deep breath, nervous, scared to remember anything else, but ready. "I turned around after looking at Sophie's front door and he was standing across the street, close to a tree. I couldn't tell if it was the same man from the bar, but it was a man, I do know that. He was leaned up against the tree smoking a cigarette, the orange blur lit brightly enough that I could see it from where I was standing. I stopped at first, debating on if I should turn around and go back into Sophie's house or if I should risk it and walk." I said, stopping for a second to take a drink of my water, officer Ivy's hand brushing up against mine as she grabbed the bottom, helping me hold it. *Wow, she has soft skin for a cop. I didn't expect that.* I thought, her fingers grazing mine before setting the water back down. My throat was finally starting to feel a little more normal and less like knives were slicing through my vocal-chords.

  "I finally decided I wasn't going to let any man keep me from walking home. It's the bad thing about when I drink, I think I'm invincible and I will prove anyone wrong who thinks otherwise….Anyway, I started walking down the sidewalk, trying to keep myself as hyper-aware as I could. I remember trying to look at him before my body was turned away from him, he wasn't wearing the same camel colored leather jacket that the guy from the bar was, but he was in jeans that looked just like the same ones that the bar guy was wearing... I only remember it because they had those tacky rhinestones on them, the ones you find near the affliction shirts in the mall." I said, instantly feeling like I could puke. I had never been a fan of those jeans, they always felt like they belonged on douche bag men and this was the perfect example of why I felt that way.

"I could hear slight footprints behind me but they were subtle. At first I wasn't sure if it was footprints or just leaves rustling across the grass in the yards next to me. At first I thought I was just being over paranoid, that I was letting the darkness, my nerves, overcome me." I said, wincing, knowing that the next part of this story was going to be hard to choke out, painful to remember. Ivy shifted her hips in the old hospital chair again, turning her head toward the hallway as we both heard someone walking.

I ignored Ivy looking away from me and kept talking, scared that if I stopped, I wouldn't be able to finish.

"I got closer to my house. In fact, I was only a few feet from my yard, when I heard footprints on the asphalt behind me. This time I knew it was feet, I could hear what sounded like boots kicking the gravel on the road." I said, starting to hyperventilate a little, my heart rate picking up speed, my pulse beating so hard I could feel it in the base of my throat. I didn't want to remember any of this, but I knew I had no choice. Officer Ivy needed to know what happened, she needed to know everything that I knew so she could find this prick.

"I started picking up speed, my strides getting a little longer, a little wider, hoping that I would get far enough away from him that I could just make it to my front porch. But I couldn't. He walked faster than I did,,Closing the gap between us quicker than I could have ever imagined…. I was scared, I didn't want to bring him close to my house. At this point it was clear he was following me. I thought if I could get far enough away from him I could call the cops but I never got that chance; until it was almost too late." I said, my voice trailing off to a whisper.

"Before I knew it, I was running, trying to escape him, making it clear that I knew he was starting to chase me. He didn't care, he kept running toward me, he wasn't stopping. I ended up at the farm that's just down the road from my house. I used to play in their pastures when I was a child, even had a few drinks there at an old bonfire party. But this was much different. I ran as fast as I could, I thought I could get away from him since I knew most of the area… I could hear him laughing, his sinister chuckles chanting behind me. He was taunting me, trying to scare the shit out of me. I wasn't going to give him the satisfaction of knowing he was scaring the death out of me. He chased me for however long it took me to get to where you finally found me. I really didn't know much about the wooded area, I have never been brave enough to go in there, even when I was a child…" I said, stopping for a moment so Ivy could finish writing what she needed to.

"I know you said that he was wearing similar clothes, just not the same jacket. Did you see anything else, did he have the same hair color, was he wearing the same shoes, anything like that?" Ivy said, looking back up at me, hoping that I had something, that I could give her, anything. Her frustration was written all over her face. I wanted nothing more than to give her whatever she needed to put that dick behind bars for good but I didn't have much.

"I never really go a super good look at his face, it was dark, pitch black other than the small glimmers of light from the moon that kept shining between the trees. When you got there, I could see a little bit more of him from your flashlight but he kept turning his face so I couldn't fully see him. I know he had brown hair, it looked similar to the guy in the bar, but his hair was all over the place. I'm sure from running. I couldn't honestly say if it was the same as the guy from the bar though…" I said in a painful, regretful tone. I wanted to be able to say that yes, they were the same man, that all they had to do was look at the security cameras, that it was going to be a simple chase, but I couldn't give her that.

"I know his general height was close to 5'10 because I am 5'6" and he was just slightly taller than me. I think he had green eyes, but I really am not sure. It was so dark, I really couldn't tell. He was white and he had a tattoo of barbed wire on one of his arms. I do know that. It looked old and similar to one that you would get in someone's house… Once again, I can't say if the guy at the bar had the same tattoo, he never took his jacket off." I said, realizing that I really didn't have anything of substance to give her. I felt defeated.

"And that prick really said something about seeing me some other time, trying to threaten me." I said, closing my eyes, wishing I could make it all go away, that it was just a bad dream I would eventually wake up from, my only relief resting in the fact that they had found him, that I had seen 3 of the officers chasing after him before I passed out unconscious. I never wanted to relive that moment, ever again.

"I guess it's a good thing your department caught him. I wish I had more information to give you so you could nail this prick to the wall, I just didn't see as much as I know you need." I said regretting every part of last night, wishing that I could give them more, that I had more information to be able to put him behind bars forever, to make him suffer like he had tried to make me suffer.

"Well, that's the issue." Officer Ivy said, turning around and sitting back down in the chair beside my bed. "We didn't actually catch him. I stopped to help you, your arm was bleeding pretty badly and I didn't want to leave you alone. I tried to take a shot at him but he kept diving and darting in different directions so I missed. Back up was there so I thought it was safe to stop and make sure you were taken care of… The other three officers that took off after him, but they lost him. We have been searching for hours but no one has found anything so far other than some foot prints and a possible direction he might have gone. The bad thing is people use those woods for hunting. It makes it hard to tell what foot prints belong to what." Ivy said, looking at me, waiting for my response. Her face was speaking volumes, the fear of the unknown circling around her. Neither of us could say another word. The room was completely silent.

03

CHAPTER

03

It felt like the walls around me were starting to close in, like the ceiling was getting closer and closer to my face. And it had nothing to do with the fact that my hospital room was smaller than some walk in closets. I could feel my heart rate speeding up faster and faster, one of the machines by my bed started chirping, officer Ivy standing up, walking toward me, placing her hand on mine.

"You have to breathe. Maybe I should come back. I don't want to overwhelm you, I knew it was too soon. I am sorry." Officer Ivy said, her hand touching the back of my hand. I took a deep breath, trying to relax, trying to calm myself down before I had a full fledged panic attack in front of the sexiest officer I had ever seen in my life. Not the look I was going for, at all.

"So what exactly am I supposed to do now exactly? He told me he would see me again soon…" I said, stopping for a second, remembering something else, my heart stopping all together.

"Officer Ivy, he knew my name, he called it out while he was chasing me." I said, starting to panic, a tear starting to run down my cheek, my body starting to feel numb. I wanted nothing more than to disassociate, to forget everything.

"He knew your name?" Officer Ivy said, writing down in her journal again.

"Yeah, when he was chasing me, he screamed it, taunting me. I was shocked. I don't know how he knew my name. I don't know if it's because he is the same guy from the bar and he heard my friends say my name, if he knew me some other way, or what, but regardless, yes, he knew my name…" I said, panic truly settling in the pit of my stomach.

"So, once again what am I supposed to do now exactly?" I said, shifting in bed and sitting up, realizing that there was a homicidal maniac running around out in the world somewhere, freely preying after someone else possibly and waiting on me to come back home.

"He knows my name. He knows where to find me. It's not like this is some big city, there isn't anywhere for me to hide. My life is here, my job is here, everything, is here, now." I said, starting to realize I had no where. I had no hiding places that I could run off to anymore.

"Do you have a boyfriend?" Officer Ivy asked, peering up from her notebook, her eye brows slightly raised.

"No, I don't date men. And this ass wipe is part of the reason I don't. Not to stereotype, but most of the straight ones are pricks." I said, trying to lighten the mood a little, chuckling.

I wasn't sure if officer Ivy was as liberal as I was. We were in the middle of nowhere Oregon, but it seemed that half of the town was either a raging homo or a raging homophobe, with really no in-between to speak of. Our town had always been divided roughly

50/50 between democrats and republicans. There was no middle man, politics at the forefront of who you spent your time with, who you chose to stick around.

"Oh... well, do you have a girlfriend you could stay with or a best friend that you could stay with, just for a few days while we patrol?" Ivy asked, a look of genuine concern on her face. It took me a second but I realized that she had separated girlfriend from best friend, acknowledging that they could be two different things. *Maybe she doesn't agree with the small town ideology they have tried to shove down our throat since we were little. hmm...* I thought to myself before answering her question.

"No, I don't have a girlfriend. And I am not staying with any of my friends right now. I am not putting anyone else at risk over this douchebag. If he comes for me and I am at someone else's house, then I am asking them to be in the middle. I am not doing that. It's too dangerous." I said, realizing I had no idea where I was going to go or what I was going to do. Normally, I would call Sophie, but I wasn't doing that right now. I wasn't dragging my best friend into the middle of all of this chaos.

My life up to this point had been a bit of a rough patch. One trial after another popping up, until I was forced into moving back home with my parents. It wasn't what I had wanted to do. I had no desire to live in my old bedroom from high school at the age of 33, and yet, after a few poor decisions, that's exactly where I had landed myself.

"I can't stay at my house, I know that. I am not letting my parents deal with this. They have done enough to help me already. My mom is already pissed at me and thinks I am a failure. I am not giving her something else to hate me for." I said, laying my head back against the hospital bed, frustration starting to build. It never failed that my life always seemed to find these dark, horrid places, lingering and hanging out there. Horrible should have been my middle name. Would have made perfect sense at this point.

"I don't know what I'm gonna do, but I will figure something out. I have no other choice, I guess." I said, panicking internally.

"Can you find my nurse? My arm is killing me." I said, looking at Ivy, her biceps pressing up against the sleeves of her police shirt as she moved, laying her notepad down in the chair as she stood up. *I guess at least if I had to almost die, I got the hot cop. Jesus, it feels illegal to be that attractive.* I thought to myself, starting to chuckle a little. *Leave it to me to have a near death experience and all I can think about is how unbelievably attractive the cop that saved me is, typical Olivia.*

"Yeah, I can get your nurse. I will be right back." Ivy said, walking towards the door, stopping at the doorframe, her hand resting on the trim of the wall, her body turning to look at me. She stopped, staring through me for a second, she was thinking something, I had no idea what it was, but, there was something there.

She turned to walk out of the room, my eyes darting to her, the way her body filled out her uniform. *She must work out, a lot. Holy shit and a half.* I thought, trying to reign back my thoughts, looking down at my scrawny arms, realizing that there were quite a few things I had failed at in life.

"Oh, hey, I was just coming to find you." Ivy said, the nurse standing in front of the doorway.

"I think I heard you say you are in some pain? I was just coming to check on you. Perfect timing." The nurse asked, walking over and checking my IV pole bags and then looking at my vitals machine, pressing a few of the buttons.

"Looks like your blood pressure is a little high too, have you been in pain for a bit?" The nurse asked, stopping beside my bed, her hand on the railing.

"Yeah, I was trying to ignore it, but it's getting pretty bad." I said, trying to wince back the pain, my arm starting to feel like it was on fire. Whatever knife he had used was sharp, very sharp, slicing my arm like it was a piece of meat.

"Okay, not a problem. Let me check your chart and see what options you have, I will be right back." She said, her ID tag flipping towards me, her name flashing quickly in front of me, Michelle. It was fitting, completely matched how she looked. She had bright red carrot top curls that she kept in a pony tail and bright pink scrubs, with a teal stethoscope around her neck, and a badge that said, 'but first coffee'.

I loved nurses, there was something incredibly attractive about them, something that lured me in, something that always seemed to drive me wild. I had dated a few nurses in the past, loving their empathy and being hooked the way they cared for people but it had never seemed to work out for whatever reason. Probably had something to do with the fact that my life always seemed to be falling apart and they dealt with enough dumpster fires at work, to want them at home also.

"Thank you, Michelle, I think it is." I said, smiling at her, flirting with her. Her cheeks starting to turn the lightest shade of pink. *She couldn't be much older than me* I thought to myself, trying to convince myself that she was in a dateable range.

She even looked like she might be a newer nurse. Judging by the way she was still smiling and didn't have giant dark circles under her eyelashes. My best guess was that she might even be gay with the way she had reacted to me paying attention to her name and picking out small details from her ID badge.

"You are welcome hun, I'll be right back." Michelle said, turning toward the door, stopping for a second when she made eye contact with Ivy. Ivy's

37

expression on her face was cold and aggressive. I hadn't seen her look at anyone like that up to this point, until now. Before Michelle walked into the room she was warm and caring. Concerned for how I was doing, but right now, she looked like she could hit someone, like she was angry.

"Oh, excuse me..." Michelle said, walking past Ivy and darting quickly through the door. Ivy sat there staring at her note pad for a little bit without saying a single word, the room filling with silence. The only audible noise was the clicking and ticking of the machines in the room.

"Is there anything else you need from me, Officer Ivy?" I asked, pulling the blankets up and over my waist, trying to stop the constant shivers that my body was starting to develop. The air conditioning blowing directly above my head, the hair on the back of my neck starting to stand straight up the colder I became.

"No, no I think that's all for now. I am going to check with your nurses and see how long they plan to keep you here for. I don't know if there is anything I or the police department can do about your living arrangement, but I will find a way to keep you safe." Officer Ivy said, tucking her notepad into the pocket of her police uniform. Her bulletproof vest pressingly tightly against her body, the muscles in her forearms flexing as she pushed the notepad further down.

"Regardless of what PD says, I will be back to check on you. I'll let you know what the plans are moving forward… Until we find this creep, you don't need to be alone." Ivy said, turning toward the door, her eyes lingering my direction.

"Okay, thanks." I said, shifting and settling down in my hospital bed. I was exhausted, my body was aching and screaming at me. I need sleep. I needed to actually rest. I was battered, bruised, every inch of my body felt like someone had taken a baseball bat to it and then run me over with an 18 wheeler for good measure.

"I am gonna try to get some rest but thank you for coming today. Just let me know what you find out, please." I said, watching Ivy walk through the door, watching the way her hips swayed as she walked, the confidence she exuded radiating from her body.

"Yeah, hopefully I will know something today." Ivy said as Michelle walked up to the doorway, waiting for Ivy to move so she could come into my room.

Ivy moved out of the way, standing in the hallway, looking into the room, lingering behind as Michelle walked over to my bedside, a little white cup in her hands with my medication.

"Here ya go. I have some medicine for you. Should help you get the rest you need. You will be out like a light shortly" Michelle said in a chipper voice, handing me the little white cup and then picking up my water jug for me, placing the straw against my lips. I looked up at her, whispering, "Thank you, miss." My eyes taking time to look at hers. Her cheeks enflaming red almost instantly again, *she is definitely gay.* I thought to myself, a slight smirk crossing my face, my gaydar was almost never wrong. I had been lesbian my entire life. Straight women were easy to spot most of the time, especially when I flirted with them. If they were truly straight, even the best flirting, wouldn't generate rosy red cheeks like Michelle had right now.

My eyes left Michelle's and turned toward the hallway, looking for Ivy, who was still standing there. Watching us from afar, the same look from before scrolling across her face. She tilted her head, nodding at me and walked off in a hurry, leaving Michelle and I alone in my hospital room.

"Interesting cop, huh?" Michelle said, chuckling, her body language screaming that she was relieved Ivy had left. "She doesn't talk much does she? Acts a bit like an ass." Michelle asked, setting the water jug down on my side table.

"I really don't know her that well. She saved my life last night, but before that I had never met her. I think she is just doing her job, but she definitely is a woman with not so many words." I said, thinking back to how she had talked to me like I was a friend, until Michelle came in the room. I was just as thrown off by her behavior as Michelle was, slightly confused as to why she was so on edge every time my nurse had come into the room. Michelle was there to do her job, to help me recover, but Ivy kept looking at her like she was a criminal or like she was jealous.

"Thank you again. Here is hoping I can get some sleep." I said, closing my eyes, flashbacks from the night before popping back into my mind, shocking my eyes back open. I had no desire to relive that night over and over, refusing to be forced to see him again.

"You are welcome. I'll come and check on you here in a bit. Try and get some rest if you can, the medicine I gave you should help. Resting in a hospital can be impossible, but with what I just gave you, you should sleep really well." Michelle said, tucking my blanket closer to me before she turned and walked out of my room. "If you need anything, I will be at the nurses station, I am just a call away, Olivia." She said and then darted down the hallway, disappearing with a quick vengeance.

I don't want to close my eyes. I don't want to see him again, I don't want to see his eyes, hear his voice. I thought, realizing that every time I closed my eyes, that's exactly what kept happening. It was like the nightmare kept appearing over and over. *What if he knows I'm here?* I whispered to myself, realizing that, the thought hadn't even crossed my mind until now. Officer Ivy had said they thought he was related to a series of killings, that this wasn't his first rodeo, *what if he tried to find me, what if he knew where I was right now? What if he had already been here?* My thoughts starting to race, starting to spiral out of control the more I was left to swim in my own thoughts, alone.

CHAPTER 04

I had finally fallen asleep, the medicine eventually kicking in. Letting my mind and body relax long enough that I could close my eyes without seeing him standing over me. Ivy's flashlight illuminating his body, leaving the outline of what appeared like a devil.

"Hey, you are finally awake?" Ivy said, standing at the doorway of my hospital room, in grey jogger sweat pants, white Adidas tennis shoes and a black, skin tight t-shirt that read 'Pivot.' across the front of it.

Her hair was down and she was wearing a light amount of make up, her entire look changing. *Wow, she is even hotter in normal clothes, how is that even possible.* I thought to myself, realizing that I was gawking at her, that I hadn't responded to her even though I had been staring at her.

"Yeah, yeah I am awake. Took that pain medicine and finally crashed. Clearly I needed it." I said, looking down at my phone, realizing that I had been asleep for over 8 hours. Sleep in a hospital was near impossible. Staff coming in and out constantly to check on you, checking vitals, looking at your IV, asking you questions, but I had been so mentally drained that I hadn't heard anyone come by at all.

"That's good. You needed the sleep. Do you mind if I sit down?" Ivy said, walking toward the chair she had been sitting in earlier, waiting for me to answer.

"Yeah, that's fine with me." I said, turning my body sideways so that it was facing her, adjusting my pillow under my cheek.

"So I talked to the chief earlier, I came by to let you know what he said at the end of my shift but they said you had fallen asleep. I guess you were screaming in your sleep at first but Michelle said you finally stopped. I didn't want to bother you so I went home to change and then came back up here." Ivy said, sitting down in the chair, her stance screaming lesbian energy. I wasn't sure if she was gay or not, maybe it was just that she was a cocky cop, or maybe it was that my gaydar was screaming at me. I really couldn't tell with her, it could go either way.

"Well, what did he say?" I asked, hopeful that he had some sort of idea, fearful of being alone. Fearful of what was going to happen when I had to leave here, terrified of what would happen to my family if I tried to come back home.

"Your nurse said they are going to discharge you tomorrow. They want to watch you overnight again, just to make sure everything is okay, since you were pretty beat up. But if everything is okay, then tomorrow morning they want to send you home. After talking with the chief, we have two options to offer you... Well, the chief has one option for you, and I have another for you." Ivy said, her voice trailing off. Her face changing slightly, she seemed a little nervous, almost.

"Chief suggested that we can have a police officer sit outside of your parents house to keep an eye on everything but I really don't like that idea. A cop can only be in one place at a time, this guy, he is intelligent, he is manipulative and if you only knew half of what he has done and gotten away with… you would understand why I hate that idea. Obviously we don't know if the guy is the same guy as the serial killer. But if he is the same person, it's too dangerous for you to go home." Ivy whispered, looking me dead in the eyes.

"And what's the other option?" I said, waiting to hear the other option, what her idea was.

"It's going to sound a bit crazy, to be honest. Chief would freak if he knew I was offering this to you, but, I couldn't live with myself if something happened to you… knowing that weirdo is still out there, roaming free and I just left you…unprotected. Anyway, I am rambling, point is, you could stay with me?" Ivy said, almost asking, almost telling me.

"I can stay with you? That's your offer? You want me to move in with someone I don't even know?" I asked, stuttering a little. Semi shocked that she had just said that. That I wasn't just dreaming. *This couldn't be real life, right?*

"Look, I know it sounds weird. Neither of us know each other, but I want to keep you safe. This asshole has possibly killed several women over the last year. You are the only one that has escaped his wrath, ill be damned if he comes back for seconds." Ivy said, her voice starting to scare me, she was being sincere, she was worried, which was driving my nerves; sending my anxiety through the roof. "At least this way, it will buy us some time. He will come back for you, there is no doubt in my mind. He is going to obsess over you getting free. It's going to eat him alive that he couldn't conquer you. He may move onto someone else, unfortunately, because he needs to kill. He needs to fuel his addiction, but eventually, when you aren't expecting it… he will find you and he will try again. I can almost promise you that." Ivy said, twisting in her chair. She was uncomfortable, she didn't want to share this information with me, but she didn't have a choice. She needed me to know just how important this was, how dangerous this situation was.

Clearly after last night, I didn't listen very well. Sophie had tried to convince me to stay and I had decided I knew what was best, ignoring her. Obviously my better judgement up to this point wasn't ideal.

"You can do whatever you want, you aren't obligated to choose either way. I just wanted you to have options, I wanted you to feel like you weren't being abandoned." Ivy said, her fingers slipping into the pockets of her joggers. The muscles above her collarbones tensing up the longer she sat there, the veins in her forearms starting to bulge slightly.

"I mean, I really don't want my parents being at risk. They have done enough for me. They don't need me bringing this shit back to their house. I should have just stayed with Sophie." I said, groaning, feeling like I was being backed into a corner. I was being faced with what felt like an almost impossible decision. I could either put my parents at risk of having some psycho try and hurt us all, or I could essentially move in with a total stranger for who knows how long.

There is no way this is real life. There is no way that my life keeps stepping off into the kind of shit that it always does. Why does weird shit like this keep happening to me? I thought, trying to figure out what to do. The inner debate in my mind, going back and forth with what decision to make.

This felt like an impossible decision, like there was no real, right or wrong thing to do. My gut instinct was saying just go home, let the cop hang out in front of my house, but after realizing that my gut was almost always wrong when it came to serious things, I wasn't sure what to do or how to feel.

"If you need time to think, I can come back in the morning, I don't mind." Ivy said, trying to be sweet, trying not to push me one way or the other.

"No, I can't let my parents be at risk. I guess I'll stay with you. Do you have a couch or something?" I asked, the words not even feeling real, even as they were leaving my lips.

"I have a spare bedroom. We can be roommates for a little bit. I won't bother you, you can do whatever you would do at your parent's house. I will just be around if you need someone and I doubt he will fuck with you if you are living with me. At least while I am there. When you leave, I will make sure you have an officer that can stay with you, if you want it. At least until we find him and apprehend him." Ivy said, standing up, stretching her body, her shirt raising slightly above the top of her sweat pants, the v-cut in her abdomen showing. *Dear lord.* I thought, trying to break my stares, my eyes refusing to look away.

"All right, I am gonna make a place for you at my apartment. I'll pick you up tomorrow once they release you. Wanna to just text me and let me know when they are planning to discharge you?" Ivy asked, grabbing her phone, opening up the phone screen and handing it to me.

"Yeah, I can do that. Weirdest way a girl has ever gotten my number before…" I said, taking her phone and putting my number into her phone, pressing dial and waiting until I heard my phone ring. Forgetting momentarily that my ringtone was set to "Move Bitch" by Ludacris. It had been a joke, Sophie had stolen my phone the night before, changing the ringtone as we were walking behind a lady who couldn't seem to move faster than the pace of a snail; laughing until she had almost peed herself. Up to this point I had forgotten she had done that, but now, with Ivy standing there, I could feel my face flashing 30 different shades of pink, landing on flaming red.

"Sorry, my friend changed my ringtone last night at the bar… Jesus, do ringtones have to be that loud?" I said, scrambling for my phone, trying to get it shut up before I dug my own grave right then and there. My ego slowly starting to deflate.

Ivy was snickering, it was the first time I had seen her laugh, seen her relax a little, it was adorable.

"No that's okay. Good song." Ivy said, walking towards my bed, grabbing her phone. "Need some water? A blanket? *Your nurse, Michelle…*"

Okay, I might be reaching, but the way she just said your nurse, Michelle, felt, jealous? No way. We don't even know each other. You clearly have had too much pain medication, you are losing it. I thought, trying not to read into everything any deeper than surface value, but she definitely had said the latter part in a much different tone.

"No, I am good. Thank you though. Seriously, thank you, for everything. I owe you, big time." I said, realizing that I hadn't really told her thank you for saving my life.

I had been so focused on other things that I hadn't expressed my gratitude to her, but I owed her my life. She really was the main reason I was still alive and breathing at this point. If she hadn't made it at the exact time she did, if she had been even a step behind, he would have killed me.

"It's what I am here for, it's my job." Ivy said, putting her phone into her pocket, turning her body away from mine. "Text me in the morning, I will swing by during my shift and pick you up. I can take you to your parents so you can get your things. Have you told them what's going on?" Ivy asked.

"Yeah, I called them. They are out of town on a trip right now. They said they were going to come back early but I told them not to. There isn't any reason for them to come back sooner, I am fine." I said, sad that I had been here alone, apart from Ivy, who had shown up like clockwork. I didn't want to call my friends, to worry them or have them come up here. There was a man on the loose who was determined to create havoc on our town, and I wasn't going to be responsible for making that any worse than it already was.

"Okay, well tomorrow I can run you by their house to get whatever you need. You can ride with me for part of the day until I can show you around my apartment, if that's okay?"

"Yeah, works for me. I have to call my work. I was supposed to be at work today but, clearly, that wasn't in the cards for me. I am supposed to work tomorrow too, but I think I am just going to call in." I said, still trying to wrap my head around the chaos that had become my life in the last 24-36 hours. It was hard to believe that just the night before I was sitting at the bar with my friends, not a care in the world, drinking and have a good time. And now I was moving in with a cop to avoid being murdered, *WTF*.

"Cool. That sounds like a good idea, I am sure they will understand, isn't every day you get chased by a murderer. Try to get some sleep tonight. See you in the morning." Ivy said, walking out of the doorway and into the hallway, waving at me as she walked away.

Could my life get any fucking weirder? I thought.

05

CHAPTER

05

"Hey, how are you feeling today?" Officer Ivy said, her voice radiating across the room from behind me. My body facing the opposite wall as I was putting on my necklace that the nurses had taken off.

I turned toward her, struggling to get my necklace to clasp. My arm starting to burn the more I tried to use it. The laceration in my bicep could not have been in a worse place.

"Like dog shit, if I am being honest. But, I am breathing, so that's something, I suppose…" I said, still fumbling with my necklace. I had spent most of the morning trying to figure out where all of my things were. The nurses trying to keep it out of my way, trying to help. But it felt like my things were scattered here there and every, pieces of the puzzle missing, my things violated by God knows who.

"Ugh, I can't get it." I said, frustrated and irritated that I couldn't get my necklace on. It was special to me, something that I never took off. My father had given it to me when I was in high school, while my parents were fighting. He had given it to me to let me know that no matter what happened, he loved me and would always be there. Regardless of, if him and my mom could fix their issues.

"Here, can I help you?" Officer Ivy asked, walking behind me, the metal handcuffs on her belt clanking. The sound of her boots causing slight flashbacks to the sound I heard from his footsteps.

"Yeah, if you don't mind. That would be great." I said, turning toward her, handing her the necklace.

"Normally I don't have an issue but right now with my arm…" I said, not even finishing my sentence before Ivy walked toward me, grabbing the necklace, her face close to mine. She looked down, tinkering with the clasp on the necklace, forcing it open and then wrapped it around my neck, her arms grazing my shoulders. Her face leaning over my shoulder to look around my neck. I could feel her breath on my skin, her chest pressing against mine, she made me nervous. A feeling I wasn't used to having with other women.

"There you go." Officer Ivy said, stepping back, smiling at me. "All better."

"Thanks." I said, still trying to catch my breath from her stealing it for a moment.

"Do you need help with anything else?" Ivy asked, her hands holding the front of her bullet proof vest. The veins in her hands gleaming under the lights as she gripped it tight. *If nothing else, she definitely has lesbian hands, that I do know.* I thought, making myself chuckle.

"Something funny?" Ivy asked, tilting her head and looking down at me. "Oh no, sorry… Just thinking, that's all." I said, embarrassed that she had heard me laugh out loud. It certainly wasn't intentional.

"And to answer your other question, no, I don't need anything else. When they brought me here all I had was what was on me at the time, not a lot to grab, I guess... They did have to get me a new shirt though, mine was ripped and disgusting." I said, looking down at the horrid hospital shirt they had given me to replace mine.

"Only thing I need is to get home so I can get my other stuff." I said, grabbing my phone off of the bed, my arm sore, bruised, throbbing. "And I guess I need to get my prescriptions from the pharmacy." I said, realizing that I wasn't even sure if my car was still in the bar parking lot or if it had been towed away by now.

"If my car was impounded, you think you can help me get it out? I had to leave it at the bar. I wasn't going to get a DUI." I said, walking toward Ivy.

"Yeah, if it was impounded, PD can help you. Clearly wasn't your fault you had to leave it there. And I would hope they would rather you walk than drive drunk." Ivy said. "I will take you to your house to get your stuff, we can go to the pharmacy before or after, your choice. Then we can stop by the bar to look for your car, if you want?" Ivy asked, walking toward the door with me. She really was sweet. Even if it was just her job, she was going above and beyond what most police officers would have done. For that, I was thankful.

"Can we go to the pharmacy first? My arm is killing me and it feels like someone ran me over with a car." I said, wincing with every movement of my arm. " Then we can stop by my parents house and I guess go look for my car after that, if that's okay?" I asked, watching Ivy walk out of the room, "We can definitely do that." Ivy said, walking toward the direction of the elevator.

"It's weird ya know. When I got here, I don't even remember making it to a room. I don't even know where I am going right now. I haven't ever been in this hospital before." I said, realizing that I had never even seen the hallway of the hospital. The walls were sterile white, a horrid floral wallpaper trim lining the middle of the wall, above the hand railing. It looked more like a nursing home than a hospital.

"Well, guess it's a good thing that I have been here several times." Ivy said, pressing the button the elevators, the dinging noise radiating through the hallway. "Need to tell Michelle bye before we leave?" Ivy said, winking at me, a smirk creeping up on her face before she walked into the elevator.

Okay, there was DEFINITELY something to that comment. Definitely. I thought, stopping for a second, enjoying the view of Officer Ivy from behind, my stomach flipping momentarily. I guess if I was going to be forced to live with a complete stranger, at least it was a ridiculously sexy cop. *Wasn't the worst thing I had done in my life…*

"Need a drink to take your meds?" Officer Ivy asked, realizing that even though we had picked up my scripts, I didn't have a way to take them.

"Yeah, if we could get something, that would be great. Or I can wait until we get to my parents house. I'm sure they have something." I said, tinkering with the buttons on the side of Ivy's cop car door. I had never been inside of a cop car, at least not in the front. It was quite a bit different then the view from the back.

"Up to you, I can do whatever. I am scheduled today but Chief knows I am helping you and said he would direct most of the calls to someone else if he could. I am at your beck and call for the moment." Ivy said, looking through the windshield, keeping her eyes fixed on the black asphalt in front of us.

"Let's just go to my parent's house. I just want to get my things and get out of there. Can you come in with me, please?" I said, hating that I felt so vulnerable, that I felt so scared. This wasn't me, I was always the type to have a 'fuck off' attitude. I was always the type that didn't get scared over anything, but at this very moment, I felt like a child, scared of the dark, scared of what was hiding in the closet.

"Yes, of course. I wasn't planning on letting you out of my sight." Ivy said, the vehicle starting to slow down, her foot pressing harder on the breaks until the vehicle stopped at the red light before my house. My eyes wandered around and out of the passenger side window, looking at the trees across the street. We were almost to Sophie's house. I felt a tinge of guilt for how things were left, felt like I needed to reach out to her but I didn't know what to say. I knew that if I told her what was going on, that she would want to be with me, that she would want me to stay with her and I couldn't do that yet, I needed to know she was safe.

We kept driving until we were close to the point that I saw him, to the place I realized I was being followed. It felt like a nightmare, all over again, but different this time.

I wasn't scared like I had been just a couple of days before, but my neighborhood felt, tattered, ruined. The place I had always felt comfort in, that had brought me peace throughout the years, now had my nerves on edge, had PTSD building in the pits of my stomach.

"It's weird, being here, after the other night." I said, watching the trees whip by. Their shadows casting on the ground as the sun beamed through them. It was a beautiful area, the ground covered in the most beautiful luscious grass. The roads lined with random wildflowers and multicolored leaves, especially in the fall. It was one of the few things I loved about living in Oregon.

"Yeah, I am sure it is. I really am sorry about what you had to go through. I couldn't imagine." Ivy said, her vehicle coming to a stop at the edge of my parents yard, her hands moving to the gear shift, placing the car in park. She turned her body toward me, looking at me with a sincerely apologetic facial expression. "I wish we could have caught him. The guys tried, but he was quick and he knew the area. He moved faster than they could and knew just the place to hide from them. I promise we will do whatever we can to find him so you can go back to your normal life." Ivy whispered, turning back toward her side of the car, her hands grabbing the latch and pulling, her door opening. She stepped out of the car, waiting on me to follow, "You coming?" She asked from outside of the car.

"Yeah." I said, grabbing the door handle, regretting having to get out of the car. I was standing right where he started to chase me, where the nightmare had truly began and it was painful. It felt like someone had punched me straight in the gut, knocking all of the wind out of my soul.

I climbed out of the car and shut the door behind me, grabbing for my keys in my jean pockets. "I won't be long." I said, walking up the front steps of my parents porch, looking down at the bushes by the front railing. Admiring my dads flowers that were getting ready to die as the weather got colder. Like all other things, even good things must come to an end at some point, might as well absorb the good while you can.

I unlocked the door and pushed it open, my parents house quiet, only the gentle noise of the heater running in the background. A slight tapping from the clock on the wall in their dining room making my body feel on edge.

"I'll wait right here." Ivy said, standing in the front entryway of my parents house, her body rigid, tense. She was holding her front bulletproof vest again, this time her biceps bulging the more alert she became. The shiny chrome from her gun reflecting into my eyes from the sun beaming down on it through the front glass door.

"I'll hurry." I said, running up the stairs in the front entry way, taking them two at a time. I didn't want to be alone. I didn't want Ivy to leave me to go upstairs by myself, but I understood why she wanted to stay downstairs, it was better for her to be by the front door, than following me. I just felt nauseated, I felt like I could vomit at any moment, my nerves were at an all time high and I felt like someone could pop out at me at any moment. Every noise in the house felt like it was 10 times louder than it really was, my anxiety climbing and growing the longer I was alone in the house.

I walked into my room with a vengeance, grabbing a bag from the top of my closet, and threw it on my bed. Unzipping it and shoving a few things here and there, I grabbed as many different pieces of clothing as I could. I grabbed my phone charger and my apple watch from my nightstand.

I hated having to pack in a hurry, I always felt like I was going to forget something and this wasn't the time for that, there was no way I wanted to have to come back here anytime soon, I wanted my parents to be safe. I didn't want that homicidal maniac anywhere near them.

I gathered the last of my stuff from my bathroom and shoved it down into my bag, taking one last glance around the room. Trying to make sure that I had what I needed to live for the next week or two, that I wasn't being too hasty.

I wasn't even sure how long I should be packing for, how long this was going to take. I hated living my life without a plan. I hated feeling like life was outside of my control, and yet, here I was, again, living life with both of them very much in the driver seat.

I zipped my bag and threw the strap over my shoulder, hoisting the back pack behind my back, realizing that most of my life was literally behind me.

Hope that's everything. I don't even really know what I need at this point. FML. I thought, jogging down the hallway. I knew I was being slightly over dramatic but I needed to get out of the house, I needed to get away from the street where my life was almost taken, I needed to find a way to breathe again.

I came flying down the stairs, refusing to look back, realizing that I still needed to get a drink before we left.

"I'm almost ready. Just need to get something to drink so I can take my meds in the car and then we can go. Thanks for coming in Ivy." I said, gripping the strap of my bag a little tighter, Ivy's face giving me comfort. Knowing she was close, that she could protect me if I needed it.

"No rush, whatever you need. I'll be right here." Ivy said, smiling at me, her beautiful teeth shining back, her dimples gleaming in the light shining through the door.

"Want anything?" I asked, turning toward the hallway that led to the kitchen. "No, I am okay." Ivy said, "but… thank you."

I finished turning around and walked down the hallway, the brightly lit sun shining through the living room windows, peering through my parents sheen curtains. I had always hated how they didn't block any of the light, that my parents living room was always lit up like a Christmas tree, until now. I was thankful at this moment, when darkness was not my friend.

I walked into the kitchen and made a bee line to the fridge, yanking on the handle and pulling the door open. I dug through the shelves, looking for something to drink that I could take with me. I knew my dad always hid a coke zero in the back from me and my mom, there had to be one in there somewhere.

I finally found a soda and grabbed it, setting it on the top of my bag, the fridge door shutting while I shimmied my stuff around, making sure it wouldn't fall.

I looked up, stopping instantly, my heart coming to a complete halt. I couldn't breathe, again.

It felt like someone had torn my lungs from my body and hung them in the air, like someone had ripped my heart out and stepped on it right in front of me.

"IVY!" I screamed, my coke zero falling to the floor, the aluminum can hitting the espresso stained hardwood floors in our kitchen, exploding, soda flying every single direction.

"What's wrong?" Ivy yelled, her boots rattling the floors as she sprinted across the house. My eyes filling with tears, my words lost in the back of my throat. Silence consuming the room, again.

CHAPTER 06

"He was here. He was in my fucking house!" I screamed, tears starting to stream down my cheeks, fear instantly settling deep into my chest.

"What do you mean? How do you know that?" Ivy asked, calmly trying to get me to answer her. "I need you to breathe Olivia, take a second and tell me what's going on." Ivy said, her face instantly going into cop mode. Her eyes darting across the room, eyeing everything, looking for something that could be out of place. Everything looked normal. Everything looked untouched, except for a little piece of paper on the fridge, with scribbled writing on it.

"Look!" I shrieked, my voice cracking, my body starting to shake uncontrollably. "He was in my fucking parent's house Ivy." I said again, struggling to speak coherently.

Ivy looked at the note that read, "You might have gotten away this time, but it won't happen again. Go ahead and stay with that little lesbian cop, she can't save you. You deserve each other. Thieves mingle with Thieves."

I stood there, refusing to believe what my eyes were seeing. Ivy instantly pressing the button on the walkie talkie that was strapped to her vest. Her words all started to blur together, the noises in the background bleeding together. I couldn't understand what they were saying, I couldn't even process my own thoughts. *What the fuck did that note even mean?!*

"I never even came to my house. I was going to try to make it to the porch but I could feel him behind me so I kept running. How does he know where I live? How did he get in here? The door was locked when we got here." I said, my mind racing, scrambling to figure out how this could have happened, thankful that my parents were out of town, that I hadn't asked them to come home early. I was scared for them to come home, scared that something would happen to them. Even if my relationship with my mom had it's flaws, I would never want anything bad to happen to her and my dad was my rock. He was always there for me, no matter what.

And they weren't who he was hunting, that was me, but he might think they were in the way. He might believe that if he hurt them, he would hurt me somehow, what if that was a part of his game, what if that is why he left me a note on the fridge. I thought, trying to make sense of everything.

"I have back up coming. Don't touch anything else. Did you touch the note?" Ivy said, pulling gloves out of her back pocket. "No, I didn't touch anything in here, besides the handle of the fridge and the inside of the fridge." I said, dropping my face into the palms of my hands, refusing to believe this was real life, refusing to believe that I was living through this horrid nightmare.

"This nightmare just began, didn't it?" I said, the room as silent as possible. The ticking from my parents clock getting louder the longer neither of us spoke. I could feel my heart beating in my ears, the colors in the room all starting to bleed together. My thoughts running in circles around the outside of my body.

Ivy turned to look at me, the note in her glove covered hands, and whispered, "Yeah."

That's all she could say, that's all she had to say to me at this moment. There were no other words she could say. I knew she didn't have the right answer, I knew that she didn't want to be honest with me. That she wished she could make this all go away, but neither of us could do that, neither of us were fucking Harry Potter.

"I need some air." I said, turning toward the backdoor, my footsteps melting into the floor, my body feeling heavy like it had in the woods.

Ivy shouted, stopping me dead in my tracks, "Wait! Don't touch the door…" Her eyes darting to the door handle, her face turning sheet white for a moment. I stopped and looked down, realizing that there was dried blood on the door handle, my hand instantly dropping down to the front of my body, my eyes bulging open once I realized what was happening.

Ivy walked over toward the door, pulling her flashlight out of her tool-belt, and flipping it on, inspecting the door handle all the way around. "Either he was bleeding when he opened the door or he had blood on his hands when he left." Ivy said, her voice slightly faltering. "You did say you talked to your parents, right?" Ivy said, stopping and looking at me, turning the flashlight off, her body language starting to change.

"Yeah, I mean I talked to them and I told them not to come home early that it wasn't important for them to do that, that there wasn't anything they could do to help me." I said, reassuring myself that they hadn't come back yet.

"But did your parents agree to stay wherever they were?" Ivy asked, putting the flashlight back into her belt, her stance becoming rigid again.

"No, not exactly. My mom told me I was being ridiculous and they could come home, but the last thing I said to her was that it wasn't necessary and then we got off of the phone." I said, still positive that they would listen to me, that they were sick of dealing with my drama and decided to stay.

"Why are you asking me this stuff anyway?" I said, naively, not piecing together what Ivy was trying to suggest.

"When you went upstairs, did you check their room? I didn't see a car in the driveway, could they have parked in the garage?" Ivy said, her breathing starting to change, her chest rising and falling a little slower.

I stopped, refusing to understand what she was saying to me, what she was trying to suggest. There was no way. There was no way that he could have done that. My parents would have listened to me, I knew them. They never parked in the garage, my dad's Land Rover was too boxy, he hated having to shimmy through the garage to get out.

"Do you want to come with me to check upstairs or do you want to stay here?" Ivy said, grabbing the side of her gun, placing her hand on the top of it, her body switching back to police officer mode.

"Well, I sure as hell am not standing down here to be murdered." I said, walking toward her, starting to panic.

"Okay, let's go. When we get up there, why don't you stay in the hallway, just to be sure. Please." Ivy said, panic rising in her voice, in her body language.

"Okay." I said, cutting my words short. I really didn't know what to say. I had nothing to say at this very moment. I was panicking, I was freaking out that my parents could be dead in the room above us and that I could have just been within 50 feet of them while I was in my room packing my stuff.

I followed closely behind Ivy, my hand grabbing the back of her leather belt, refusing to let go. My fingers intertwining underneath her belt loop until I was practically attached to her. We walked up the stairs, my feet refusing to walk normal, my body starting to lose control. My heart was pounding in the base of my throat.

We reached the top of the stairs after what felt like an eternity, her boots stepping onto the carpet at the top of the walkway, her body slowly walking forward, her hand never leaving her gun. She was looking at everything. Her eyes scanning the walls adorned with my childhood photos on the wall, our family photos, pictures of my parents when they were first married. Looking at the few photos we had of my brother from when he was a toddler and several photos of me with different friends, at sporting events, pretty much every moment from my childhood.

"I can't do this Ivy." I whispered, the photos of my parents, of me growing up, igniting tears, sending me into a full blown panic attack.

"Hopefully they stayed away, I just want to check. Just want to make sure. The blood had to have come from somewhere." Ivy said, stopping before she reached my parents door, her body tensing up, her feet planting themselves to the floor.

"Why did we stop?" I said, my head jammed up against the back of Ivy's back. I was scared to look. I was scared to see anything that could be down the hallway, I didn't want to face whatever we might stumble upon.

"I'm not sure. Can you see what I can see?" Ivy said, trying to turn toward me, my body tucked behind hers.

"No. I can't and I don't want to. Just tell me what it is." I said, acting like a child, behaving like a two year old. I couldn't force myself to stand up and look forward. I couldn't bare to see my parents dead.

"Well, the door handle is covered in blood like the door handle downstairs…. And there is another note on the door, with your name on it." Ivy said, her words fading away as I felt my soul starting to leave my body.

"What did you just say?" I asked, finally regaining my nerve for a moment, my worlds stumbling out of my mouth like my drunk walk home the other night. *We should have checked the garage.*

"Hold on." Ivy said, pulling away from me, grabbing the black leather gloves from her back pocket again, putting them on her hands. I stood up straight, finally acknowledging what she had said, finally deciding that I had to be an adult. I had to stop acting like a child and face what was going on, what my new reality had become.

I heard the front door open, a strange mans ringing through the hallway, "Carlton PD. Ivy you here?"

"Yeah, upstairs. Check the downstairs. Look in the garage for a car!" Ivy shouted, her gloved hands reaching for the taped note off of my parents door, my eyes realizing that there were little blood spots all across my parents bright white floors. I started to feel my heart sink to the floor, my entire life felt like it was coming to a complete halt, this couldn't be happening. I had been in such a hurry to pack my bags that I hadn't stopped to notice any of this. I had been in my own little world, obviously.

Ivy flipped the folded note open and started reading it out loud, "Olivia, want to play a game...? In the hospital you wanted to know how I knew your name, oh, but you are the one to blame. Memories will come and memories will go, my presence will never leave you though..." Ivy whispered, her voice trailing toward the end of the sentence. She stopped, folding the paper back, my mind racing, trying to figure out who could hate me so much that they could do this to me, that they could want to create this much fear.

"Open the door Ivy." I said, taking a deep breath, preparing myself for whatever was behind the closed door, for whatever I was about to see.

Ivy grabbed the door with her gloved hands and shoved it open, both of our breaths stopping for a moment, our eyes darting around the room, the empty room, with a perfectly made bed.

"There is another note." I said, sprinting to the bed, regaining my strength as I realized my parents weren't laying in their beds dead or on the floor.

"You got lucky, again. Two strikes. We won't make it to three." I said, reading the card out loud, Ivy stepping behind me and grabbing the card with her gloved hands.

"So who the hell's blood is all over my parents doors?" I shouted, starting to unravel, my mind holding on by a thread.

"I don't know. But we are going to find out." Ivy said still scanning the room, making sure we hadn't missed anything, "Oh and Olivia, I know you are stressed and worried, but next time, let me touch everything. We need every bit of evidence we can get on this guy. If you get your fingerprints on anything, that's going to make this process longer. I promise I am not trying to be a dick. I just want to stop this asshole, I want him to be put behind bars." Ivy said, placing the card with the other notes she had in her police uniform.
"Ivy, coast is clear downstairs, no car in the garage!" A man's voice shouted from underneath us.

Ivy turned toward the door, "Let's go downstairs, I need to tell the other guys what we found up here. I am glad their car wasn't here."

"Yeah, I know." Ivy said, standing in a circle of police officers, including the police chief, who looked highly concerned, his mustache furrowing; his teeth clenching on the inside of his cheek, chewing nervously.

I was sitting in a chair at the table in my parents dining room, trying to regain my sanity as best as possible, barely listening to anything that the police officers were talking about. I didn't have the energy to hear any more bad news for one day, I just couldn't bare anything else.

I tried to call my parents but they weren't answering. I left a voicemail explaining for them to call me as soon as they could and preferably before they came home. I didn't want the first thing that they saw when they drove up to be police tape and freak out. I didn't want them to have to go through anything that I had been through over the last 48-72 hours. My life was starting to feel like an episode of 48 hours at this point, one horrible discovery after the next. Missing puzzle pieces laying, scattered everywhere, leaving no real clues as to what was going on.

"Want to get out of here? We got everything we could. Chief Roberts is going to send everything off to forensics. See if we get any hits, if anything comes back. But for now, there isn't anything else we can do here." Ivy said, adjusting her belt.

"Yeah. I guess." I said, standing up, my legs starting to feel like jello. My arm was radiating pain from my shoulder blade down to my fingertips, I had never had a chance to take my pain medication and I was starting to feel every bit of it, the nerves in my arm on fire.

"I tried to call my parents but they aren't answering the phone. I left them a voicemail to call me back when they could. I just don't want them driving up to this nightmare." I said, wincing as I put my jacket back on, my arm feeling like it could fall off.

"Here, let me help." Ivy said, holding my jacket so I could put my arm into one side and then the other, her body rotating to the front of my jacket, grabbing the zipper, lining it up and helping me zip it right above my breasts. She didn't mean anything by it but her fingers had grazed my chest as the zipper was sliding up, goosebumps trailing across my arms and legs. Her face looking down at mine, her lips pressed together, perfectly shaped. She was definitely gorgeous.

"Let's get out of here. I think you have had enough for one day. Let's go find your car." Ivy said, putting her hands in her pockets, her stance changing again. She had been more relaxed while she was helping me put on my jacket, flirty almost, but it changed as soon as another cop walked past us, she jerked back into police officer mode.

"Yes, please." I said, walking toward the front door, relief overcoming my body as I realized I didn't have to worry about staying here alone tonight, that I had somewhere safe I could hide, that Ivy would be there to protect me.

CHAPTER 07

The car ride to the bar was extremely quiet. I had nothing more to say, I didn't even know where to begin. All I could do was look out of the car window, looking at all of the trees, watching the leaves flutter in the wind, my heart wanting to stop beating. I was exhausted. I was completely emotionally drained. I couldn't take anything else. I needed a reprieve, I needed this asshole to be caught already.

Ivy didn't speak either. The only noise in the background was an inaudible murmur from her police walkie talkie, the gentle whisper of other police officers being summoned for some other disaster in town.

"I don't know how you do this every day." I said, still looking out of the window. Focusing on the yellow stripes of the road flickering as our car lights hit them, the sun starting to set, the sky turning a burnt orange and purple color, snow clouds starting to linger in the sky.

"Well, I don't do THIS every day." Ivy said, shifting her hands on the steering wheel. "It's not every day that Carlton has a serial killer to deal with, but it is part of the job. I signed up to protect, to make sure that the people in this community were safe, and that's what I do. That's how I do it. I remind myself constantly that my main priority is the people in this town."

"I get that, but, how do you go to sleep at night? How do you see all of this bad stuff happening? Face it head on, and are still capable of closing your eyes at night?" I asked, realizing that what I was feeling right now, that what I was fearing every time I closed my eyes, was Ivy's every day reality. It was her normal, her necessity.

"You get used to it, I guess. You learn that if you don't, it will consume you. Drive you mad. But, to be honest, there are still times that I am human. There are still times that I see things I wish I could burn from my mind, that I could have gone without." Ivy said, pain flickering in her eyes. I didn't know what all she had seen and I wasn't sure if I wanted to know, if I wanted to have even a glimpse into what she had endured over the last few years as a cop.

"I don't think I could ever get used to it. I don't think I could ever stop looking over my shoulder. I think your job would put me in a psych ward." I said in all sincerity.

I wasn't cut out for this. I was a newspaper editor, I liked to write and edit. I liked hiding behind a good book, living a simple life. Doing my job and going home. I had already tried the high class action type of job and it wasn't for me, it was too much for me to handle, made me drink more and more every day that I had to go into work.

"I guess I am luckier than I thought working at the newspaper here. I always thought I had a boring job, that I wanted to do more, that I wanted to be more. But now, I am just glad that my job now is pretty mundane." I said, chuckling, internally trying to think of myself as a cop, that was a joke. I could never, would never.

Ivy laughed, her eyes looking over my direction as she came to a stop at the light in front of us. She had an adorable laugh. She had a laugh that I would not have expected her to have, it was very feminine, very cute. It definitely didn't match her personality or her physique. But it made her unique, which I liked, it was different, unexpected.

"Looks like Larry left your car alone." Ivy said, her forearm pressing against the steering wheel, her pointer finger pointing toward the bar parking lot, my black range rover sitting in the parking lot.

"Wait, how did you know what I drive?" I asked, stopping for a second, looking at her, waiting for an answer. My eyes scanning the parking lot, looking at all of the other cars in the parking lot.

"I'm a cop, Olivia. When I ran your license to identify you, I can see quite a bit about you. Even the DUI you had a few years ago." She said, her voice trailing off. "Is that why you walked home?" Ivy asked.

"Yeah…" I said, embarrassed and caught off guard that she could see that on my record. I should have known that she would know, that I couldn't hide it. She was a cop for gods sakes but at the same time, it felt like a small invasion of privacy, knowing that Ivy could see parts of my life I tried to hide from everyone else. I had done everything in my power to hide that I had gotten a DUI, refusing to tell hardly anyone. When people had asked why I came back to Oregon, I just told them that I needed a change of pace, that I was over the hustle and bustle.

Ivy parked her police car beside mine, unclasping her seatbelt and letting it slide back against the trim of the car. "Look you don't have to worry, I only found what I needed to find. I stopped looking once I got what I needed. I only saw your DUI because it populated under most recent concerns." Ivy said, her fingertips tracing the stitching in her steering wheel.

"No that's okay. It's a part of my past, part of why I am back at my parents house and it's entirely the reason that I am working at the Carlton News instead of the New York Times. I had everything, I had the 'perfect' job, I had the perfect friends and I ruined it all. Lost everything and came back home." I said, trying to be as vague as possible. Not wanting to open up to a strange cop, at least not yet. I wanted to know her before I disclosed these things. I hadn't even really told Sophie what happened, I didn't want her to judge me, to think I was a bad person.

"You don't have to tell me anything you don't want to tell me, Olivia. How about you let me warm up your car real fast and then you can follow me back to my apartment? I was going to head back to the station and swap out for my car, but it's getting late and my shift ended a few hours ago. I would rather head home, change and find something to eat. You good with that?" Ivy said, opening her door and reaching her hand toward me, my heart skipping a beat. I looked at her hand, confused, reaching my hand toward hers, slowly moving it, not sure if she was trying to hold my hand or what was happening.

"Keys?" Ivy said, shivering. The wind hitting her back. *Wow, I am a freaking idiot.* I thought, scrambling to get my keys out of my jeans.

"Here ya go." I said, handing my keys to her so she could start my car. I had never had someone turn my car on for me, much less turn it on so they could make sure it was warm. Her kind heart was refreshing, something I wasn't used to, and I had just tried to embarrass the hell out of myself by thinking she wanted to hold my hand. *Great.*

I watched Ivy walk to my car, opening the door, turning the car on, her hands floating to the switches for the heat. She sat there, blowing warm air into her hands, her legs hanging out of the passenger seat, her body leaning against the console in the middle of my car.

I couldn't take my eyes off her, I wanted to watch her. I wanted to memorize her every move.

She had a tattoo down her left forearm, something that I hadn't paid much attention to before, it said resilience in beautiful black writing, elegant. She had another tattoo behind her left ear, it was a small black cross, very hip. I liked that she was different, she certainly wasn't like any of the rest of the crowd I had been around my entire life. I had always been friends or dated people that were either very rustic or very refined, and nothing in-between, maybe that was part of the issue.

Ivy hopped out of the car, looking into the back seat, scoping things out and walked around the car. She opened every car door to inspect, making sure that no one was in there waiting on me. It made my heart flutter, her attention to detail, the way she cared, the size of her heart, you could see it, you could feel it in every action she made.

"All right, we are all clear. Your car is pretty warm now. Wanna follow me to my apartment?" Ivy said, smiling. "And maybe at some point, you can hold my hand if you would like?" Ivy said, winking at me, my faces instantly flushing bright red, she had caught on to my slip up earlier. I felt like the nurse at the hospital, my ears turning the same color as the red light on top of her cop car.

"You saw that." I said, not sure how to even overcome at this point.

"Yeah. But I can't say I haven't thought about it, myself." Ivy said, closing her door, my eyes following her around the front of the cop car, her hand reaching for the handle of my door.

83

She opened my car door for me and waited, turning her body and opening the door to my range rover. I climbed out, in shock. I had never had someone open my car door for me, it was an abnormal feeling, having someone cater to me like this.

"Thanks." I said, awkwardly walking away from the car, Ivy shutting her police door shut and waiting at the door of my SUV.

"You are very welcome. Let's go home." Ivy said, her voice calming, serene.

Home, where was home even at, now. I thought to myself, the car door shutting, my fingers instantly reaching for the lock button, pressing it down, the locks snapping aggressively into the door, a sense of relief sweeping over me. This was the first time in several days that I had been anywhere that was mine that hadn't been invaded. The first time I had been able to touch something without panicking that it had been molested by some psychopath.

I watched Ivy back her car out, her wheels turning against the white pavement rocks, a cloud of dust following her car. I put my car in reverse, backing up, and then pulled forward, following behind her, leaving the bar where it all started in my rear view mirror.

We drove for several miles, my thoughts weaving and drifting into the air. My mind hurt, my brain felt like it was going to explode. My body was sore. Everything just felt like it was slowly falling apart at the seams, Ivy being the only thing holding any of it together still.

There was something special about her, she was gentle, but yet, a hard-ass. On the exterior, from afar she looked like she could knock you out, straight KO you. But once you got to know her, once you saw the other sides of her, what was inside, it was gentle, sweet, empathetic and passionate.

The weird thing is whoever this douchebag is, he said something about Ivy being a lesbian and that she couldn't protect me. Was whoever he was, right? Was she really a lesbian, how did he know that? I had so many questions running through my mind. I was assuming she was gay based on her comment about holding my hand, but people can fool you. *You really need to stop thinking about Ivy like it's a good time to find someone to date. Get it together Olivia.*

The wheels of my brain changed gears. Turning over and over, constantly going through everything he had said to me, both, verbally and written on creepy notes. I couldn't stop thinking, couldn't move past everything that had happened over the last couple of days.

I watched Ivy's brake lights illuminate in front of me, the sky had turned completely dark. Her car rolling to a stop, her turn signal on, pointing toward the high end apartment complex.

Is this where she lives? I thought to myself, expecting something much different, expecting a small house in the woods; somewhere, a little less 'posh' and a little more modest.

I didn't care if she had a 'posh' place or a small cottage, or even a giant mansion. After my life experiences, money didn't mean near as much to me as it had before. I changed substantially after my DUI, my attitude on life, morphing out of desperation, being forced to change, whether I wanted to or not.

I just was surprised that she lived in these apartments. These were the apartments that the doctors, attorneys, and any other high class person close to Carlton lived in. When I was moving back, I had checked the prices, hoping that I could afford them and quickly realized that these flats were well above my pay grade. There was no way I could afford these working for the newspaper. Hell, I didn't even know if I could afford them when I worked for the New York Times, $2,500 a month for a one bedroom loft was steep, too rich, even for my blood.

I watched Ivy's car pull into a parking place in the garage of her apartment, the headlights shining against the giant concrete wall, my car following behind, parking in the spot next to where she had just pulled her car in. I gathered up my things, pulling the mirror down, looking at my face. I looked pitiful, my hair was a mess, my mom bun threatening to come apart, little hairs flying all over my head, deep dark circles starting to form under my eyes. *I'm starting to look like I have shriveled up ball sacs under my eyes, cool. If this guy doesn't take me out soon, he probably should, I look dead anyway.* I thought to myself, my dark sense of humor starting to come out.

My therapist had been telling me that a dark sense of humor was fine, but not if it was masking the real problems in life, if it was being used as a coping mechanism. She might have been right, but at this moment, with everything going on, I really didn't care. Right or not, she wasn't living in my life, she wasn't standing in the fiery pits of hell that I was currently. I really didn't give a shit if she thought I shouldn't be covering up my insecurities with dark humor at this very moment.

I grabbed my chapstick from the cupholder of my car, pressing it against my lips, my lips pressing together, forcing the moisture into my skin. *I need a shower and desperately.* I thought, realizing that I hadn't taken a shower in almost 3 days. I had to smell similar to the dumpster we were parked by at this point.

Great, smelling real hot for the sexy cop right now, cool. One more thing to remind me just how wonderful my life really is right about now. I thought, tossing the chapstick back into my cup holder. A tap on my driver side window startling me back to reality. Ivy was standing there, waiting on me, her arms shivering.

She was still in her police uniform, which wasn't very thick, her jacket still at the office.

"Shit. I'm sorry. I didn't realize you had gotten out of your car yet." I said as I opened the door, Ivy's body between both of our vehicles, her hands perched on the straps of her vest again. The veins in her arms bulging even more than before, my eyes looking her up and down. *Maybe having to stay in Ivy's spare room won't be so bad, at least it has a nice view.*

"That's okay, I just wanted to make sure you were okay. Come on, I will show you where to go." Ivy said, turning around and walking behind the cars, waiting on me, patiently. I locked the car door relentlessly, the honking noise echoing throughout the garage over and over.

"I'm sure that was overkill, but after everything lately, I just want to make sure it's locked." I said, trying to hide my embarrassment. I was sure I was being ridiculous, that locking the car over and over wasn't actually going to make it more locked than before, but it made me feel better, more secure.

"I get it. Completely." Ivy said, walking a few steps ahead of me to the elevators.

"Well, this is fancy." I said, watching Ivy press the buttons to the elevator.

"Yeah, I guess so. It's close to the police station, close to my gym, close to coffee shops. Over priced though." Ivy said, acting nonchalant, like it wasn't any big deal she lived here, stepping back so she was behind me, my body in front of hers.

The elevator doors opened, a random person who lived at the apartments popped out of the elevator. I jumped, a knee jerk reaction from the PTSD of the last 48 hours. Ivy placed her hand on the small of my back, her hand reminding me she was still there, that I wasn't alone. "It's okay, they live here." She whispered, guiding me into the elevator, her hand still on my back.

"Sorry. I just got spooked. Wasn't expecting anyone to be getting off the elevator. I'm a little jumpy right now." I said, my cheeks starting to flush from awkwardness. "That's okay, you don't have to apologize. I don't blame you for being jumpy right now." Ivy said, reassurance in her voice.

There was something about her that calmed me, that reminded me that I was still alive and that maybe, just maybe, life would be okay. I felt at peace around her, I felt like I was in safe hands. Whether she meant to or not, the little things, like placing her hand on my back, or stepping behind me, they all meant something, they all made me feel sheltered.

The elevator finally reached the top floor, the doors opening to a lit hallway on the inside of the building. "You live on the top floor?" I asked, realizing this was the penthouse suite. The floors were lined with the most beautiful white granite, with grey striping throughout. The walls were lined with embossed wallpaper that I could only imagine was special ordered. Her door was massive, taking up over half of the wall, the woodgrain of the door looked like tiger striping, something I had never seen before.

"Jesus, this is beautiful." I whispered, feeling slightly inadequate. "I uh, I could never afford this place." I said, Ivy's hand reaching in her pockets for her key card. *The doors even have special locks, wtf. Talk about bougie.* I thought to myself, gripping my bag against my shoulders, my fingers tugging tighter.

"It's okay, I guess. I like it, for now. Eventually I want to build my own place, but I wanted to make sure I wanted to keep living here. Didn't want to jump the gun." Ivy said, pushing the door open and walking in, tossing her key card on the illuminated cut out in the wall specifically designed to be an entry table. The walls were covered in the same beautiful granite that the floors were, the ceilings were vaulted and massive, exposed ventilation throughout, the opposite wall composed of different colored bricks. I looked up and realized that the entire wall facing across from me was covered in glass overlooking downtown. Carlton downtown wasn't anything special, it looked just like every other small town downtown living, but the view was still beautiful nonetheless. The lights from the shops and the lights of the cars were twinkling through the glass.

Ivy had a beautiful caramel colored leather couch and two darker colored leather chairs sitting in her living room. A beautiful boho chic black and white rug was sitting underneath a modern metal coffee table. I walked over to the couch, sitting my bag down, taking everything in, realizing there was a double sided fire place in the back corner of the room that shared both the living room and the dining room.

"Wow. Your place is stunning." I said, turning around and looking into the kitchen, the dark black cabinets standing out, the flat black handles on the cabinet doors peaking my interest. I walked over to the kitchen, letting my fingers touch everything, her place was spotless, there wasn't a speck of dust on anything. I stopped, looking up to find Ivy, who was standing in front of the giant island in her kitchen, watching me.

"Thanks. It isn't bad. I'm glad you like it." Ivy said, taking off her vest and laying it in one of her white leather barstools. "I really don't spend much time here, I prefer to be outside." Ivy said, walking over to the fridge. "Want something to drink? I have water, tea, soda, or wine? I think I might even have some coffee if you prefer that." Ivy said, digging around, looking for something that she wanted.

"I'll take some water, if that's okay. But if you have some coffee, I'll probably want some of that later or in the morning." I said, realizing that if I was going to be staying here, I needed to purchase a few things. I hadn't thought about just how much my life was about to change, until now. I hadn't had time to think about anything after the events from the last couple of days, my life was in shambles and I didn't even know how to start picking up the pieces.

"I can definitely have some coffee for you in the morning. Here…" Ivy said, handing me a bottle of water from the fridge. "I'm gonna have some wine, if you want some, the offer still stands." Ivy said, grabbing a glass from one of the cabinets beside the sink.

"So, you know there is no way I can pay half of the rent, right?" I said, regretting that I even had to speak the words. But there was no way I could afford this, I wasn't even sure how much it was a month, but it was well over what I had been paying at my parents, which was nothing.

"I didn't expect you to pay anything." Ivy said, looking up and making eye contact with me while she was pouring herself a glass of moscato. "I offered because I want you safe. This place is locked down like Fort Knox, the only way in here is with a key card." Ivy said, tilting her glass toward her lips, letting the wine drip down her throat. I could see a sense of relief wash across her face as the wine hit her blood stream, her body starting to relax.

"Come on, I'll show you to your room." Ivy said, grabbing her glass of wine, walking toward me, her body getting insanely close, her arm wrapping around my body, her face almost touching mine. She grabbed her vest from the barstool I was standing next to and then stepped back, grinning at me before she walked around me. I could feel my face flushing, my breathing slowly stopping for a moment. For a second, I thought she was going to kiss me, that she was leaning in so she could get close to me, but I was wrong. I didn't realize that she was trying to get her vest or that I was blocking her from doing so.

Ivy walked around me and the island to the other side of her kitchen, a little hallway tucked behind the kitchen, the giant wall of windows lining all the way down the hallway. We passed by the first door, "That's your bathroom, it's a little small but it will do the job." Ivy said, my head turning to look, *that's her idea of small?* I thought, realizing that our ideas of small were very different. The bathroom was massive, a gigantic and lavish shower against the wall, floor to ceiling glass protecting the black and white tiled floors. There was a floating espresso stained vanity up against the wall and a toilet nicer than my car up against the opposite wall.

"I think it will work just fine." I said, in complete shock. Ivy kept walking, pointing to the next door, "That's my gym, there isn't much in there, a few weights, a stationary bike, a treadmill, just basic stuff. You are welcome to use any of it if you would like while you are here." She said, continuing to walk in front of me, my mouth open far enough it felt like my jaw could hit the floor at any moment.

Ivy stopped at the next door, "This is my room and yours is at the end of the hall. Do you want me to show you around or do you want to look at it alone?" Ivy asked, stopping in front of her door.

"I can look around, why don't you change. I am sure you can't be comfortable in that uniform." I said, realizing that she had been wearing her uniform for well over 12 hours by this point.

"Yeah, it's the worst part of the job, honestly." Ivy said, chuckling. "Cool, well I am gonna take a quick shower and change. If you need to shower or anything, there are fresh towels in your bathroom and you are welcome to use whatever you need to, make yourself at home" Ivy said, opening her door and stepping inside of the doorway. "And if you need anything, I am just in here. Find me if you need anything at all, I'll be out in just a few minutes. Maybe we can find something to eat?" Ivy said, starting to unbutton her top, the top of her shoulders exposed, the muscles in her neck and shoulders gleaming from under her police shirt.

I couldn't speak, I was mesmerized by the muscles covered across her body. I could feel myself staring, watching her unbutton each individual button, pulling on the bottom of her shirt until it wasn't tucked into her pants anymore, my eyes lingering until she started tugging on her belt. *STOP STARING OLIVIA.*

"Okay, if I need anything I will let you know. I am gonna take a shower too. I will try to hurry, but I need to wash the last few days off. Food sounds amazing though." I said, trying to act normal, trying to play off the fact that I was very attracted to her.

"See you soon." Ivy said, slowly shutting the door as I turned to walk toward the room she said I could stay in. I pushed on the huge door, letting it open, a massive room standing in front of me.

There was a giant perfectly made king bed up against the wall covered in the most beautiful black bedding, a fuzzy white fleece blanket folded up perfectly and draped across the corner of the bed. I stood at the doorway scanning the room, looking at the opposite side of the room, a massive flat screen tv mounted to the wall, a beautiful modern gold desk up against the wall under the tv. *She has fantastic taste, I will say that. I have never seen an apartment this nice in my life, even when I lived in New York.* I thought, feeling very inferior.

I had always lived a mostly modest lifestyle, apart from my car. I loved my car. I had worked hard to earn enough money to buy it, paying cash after saving for years. Before my DUI I hadn't been able to save anything, spending money faster than I could make it. Racking up debt on every credit card that they would let me take out. My credit taking a nose dive before I even hit the age of 25. I was living like I had money running out of my ears, like debt wasn't an issue.

Unfortunately, as time went on, the debt started mounting and even with my high paying New York job, I couldn't afford the lifestyle I was leading. I was starting to drown, writing non stop for the New York Times trying and failing to keep up. Chasing after every girl I could find, drinking daily, hoping it would cover up the pain I was feeling, hoping it would fill the void I had. I refused to allow myself to feel real feelings, I refused to let myself see that I was the problem. I wanted to run from my problems, I wanted nothing to do with responsibility.

I kept leading that life for as long as I could. Drinking day in and day out, until it finally caught up with me. I had been out with work friends on a Friday night. Drinking shot after shot, tossing one drink back and instantly ordering another. By the time I left the bar I was so drunk I couldn't even remember where I had parked my car. I was stumbling on the sidewalk, tripping over my own feet, dropping my keys every other step. I should have never gotten into a car, I should have stopped right then and there and ordered a taxi, but I was invincible, I didn't need any help.

That night, I made the worst decision I could have ever made. I stumbled up to my car, fumbling with my keys, trying to get the car unlocked. After what seemed like an eternity, I crawled into the car and threw it in drive, darting out of the parking lot. I don't remember a lot after that, except waking up in a hospital, a police officer standing outside of my room, but this time it wasn't because I had been in danger, it was because I had been the danger.

I hated remembering that night, I wanted nothing more than for it to just go away, but it wouldn't. I still had nightmares, little pieces of that night coming back in waves, rolling in and rolling back out. It was one of the worst nights of my life.

I ended up losing my job, after the paper found out. My boss told me that I couldn't work there anymore, that they didn't want the face of their paper to be a raging alcoholic. They needed someone doing my job to be reputable, to be believable and honest, something that I clearly was not.

I couldn't really blame them, they had a reputation to protect and I was threatening that. I was putting their name on the line. I was the writer that they had turned to when they needed a high profile story investigated, when they wanted someone they could trust and I was steadily becoming the opposite.

It was that day that I realized I needed help. I needed to come back home. I didn't have a choice, I didn't have any real friends in New York. Most of my friends had dumped me after my DUI. I had lost my job, and I was already drowning in debt. I had backed myself into one hell of a corner, digging my own grave.

I eventually called my parents and told them what happened. They were disappointed and gave me the lecture of a lifetime. My mother more so than my father, but they still were there for me. They ended up coming to New York, helping me pack up my life and placing it in the back of their Land Rover.

It felt like the end of my life but it was really just the beginning. I couldn't see that at the time but after multiple sessions with my therapist, I started to see that it was the best thing that could have ever happened to me, that I needed a life wake up call.

The irony of it all is that the wake up call I needed was so I didn't end up dead and here I was, running for my life, again, just in a different way. Trying not to die.

08

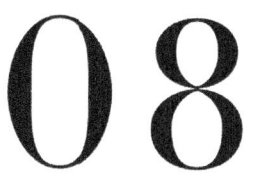

CHAPTER

08

"My parents finally called me back. I told them what was going on and what had happened to their house. My mom is panicked, she doesn't want to come home. I really don't blame her." I said, taking a bite of the fries Ivy had door-dashed for us. "My dad said that he wanted to come home, that he wanted to be here so he could protect me, but I think mom has convinced him that they would be better off staying out of town for a few more days, just to see if you all have any leads."

"Yeah, it's probably best they stay away from here for the moment. I know they can't stay away forever, but until we get the lab results back, I think it's a good idea that your mom pushed for them to not come back just yet." Ivy said, picking at her burger. She had a look on her face that was screaming concern.

"And I tried to call Sophie but she didn't answer. I texted her but no response either. I guess she is still mad at me." I said, staring at my food and then looking back up at Ivy, who still hadn't taken a bite to eat.

"Not hungry?" I asked, trying to change the subject. Ivy had been playing with the same part of her burger for several minutes, hardly touching her food. I could tell she was thinking something but she wasn't hardly saying a word.

"No, I am hungry. I just have a lot on my mind. I want to catch this guy, I need to catch him" Ivy said, finally taking a small bite from her sandwich, her jaw clenching down with each bite.

"What do you think is going to happen? Like really? I mean I can't hide in your apartment forever and my parents can't stay on vacation for an unlimited amount of time. Eventually I have to go back to work, they have to come home... but if he is still out there, how are we even supposed to keep living..." I said, almost rhetorically. I knew Ivy didn't have the answers, there really weren't any answers at this point.

"To be honest, I really don't know what we are going to do, but I do know that I promised to keep you safe and that's what I am going to do." Ivy said, looking up, her eyes meeting mine, her legs propped up in her dining room chair, her arms wrapped around her legs.

"How about we try to figure some of this stuff out tomorrow, when we both have had some sleep?" Ivy said, dropping her feet to the floor and sliding to the edge of her chair.

"Yeah, you are right. I am overthinking, again." I said, taking one last bite of my fries, standing up and walking toward the kitchen. "Where is your trashcan?" I asked, realizing that it was going to take me a while to figure out where everything was. I was in a foreign place, unknown territory.

"It's beside the fridge, in the pantry, on the floor." Ivy said, standing up from the table, following me to the pantry. "Yeah,. there." Ivy said as I pointed to the door, motioning to make sure that's what she was talking about.

"I wish I had the right answers and I might have better ones tomorrow. I am just exhausted, today has been a bit draining." Ivy said, throwing her half eaten plate of food in the trash.

"You aren't lying." I said, following her lead and throwing the rest of my food away.

"I just hope I can sleep." I said, stopping at the kitchen island again, propping my arms across the cold marble counters. "I haven't really been sleeping much. The meds help, especially with my arm, but idk if these are strong enough to help me like they did in the hospital." I said, wincing at the thought of having to lay my head down, at the thought of having to close my eyes again.

"I can't promise everything will be okay, but I can promise that myself and the rest of the police department are trying to find this guy. The biggest issue we have right now is we don't know if he is the same guy from the bar... Is he the same man that's been killing women around this area for over a year, or is he someone completely different. He is a mystery at this point. Once we have an idea of who he is, things should be more clear." Ivy murmured. "I know that talking about this right before you go to sleep probably isn't the best idea though. How about we talk about this in the morning?" Ivy asked, walking toward me, her body turning, her legs jumping until she landed on the counter to sit down beside me.

"Yeah, I probably shouldn't talk about any of this right now, but it's all I can think about. It's consuming my thoughts." I said, Ivy's thigh brushing up against my forearm, the hair on my arms standing up straight.

"Well, I'm off tomorrow, I called chief and asked if I could take a personal day. I didn't want to leave you alone and I figured that at least for tomorrow, me being here, was for the best. How about once you get up in the morning, we sit down and write down what we do know, maybe see if we can figure out any clues that might help while we wait on the forensics report to come back?" Ivy asked, scooting her leg closer to my arm, her leg resting against my skin. I wasn't sure if she was doing it on purpose or not, but she had every one of my senses about to lose control. She made me exceptionally nervous. She made my heart flutter and my stomach do back flips.

"Yes, let's do that. Maybe talking through it and writing it down, we can come up with something together." I said, moving my arms further in front of me, resting my face against the cool marble. My hair flinging every which direction, my shirt raising in the back, the cool draft in the room penetrating the skin on the small of my back.

"Perfect." Ivy said, her feet dangling from the counter, one of her feet grazing my thigh. I felt an instant rush of goosebumps forming on my arms, running down my body to my legs as her foot brushed up against my skin. I kept laying in the same position, hoping that she would get closer to me, that she would make a move, hoping that I wasn't just over reading the situation.

Ivy jumped off of the counter, startling me, my body lurching upright almost immediately. "All right, well it's late. Why don't we both try and get some rest." Ivy said, walking around the island to the hallway leading to our rooms.

"Yeah, you're right. Rest would probably be good for both of us. I'm just gonna take my medicine and i'll be down there in a moment." I said, turning to the fridge to get another water. "Also, tomorrow I will get some groceries. I don't want you to think that I am taking advantage of you." I said, fishing for a water bottle behind the other drinks in her fridge.

"Don't worry about that. I have plenty of stuff and I needed to place an order soon anyway. I will do that in the morning." Ivy said, standing at the beginning of her hallway.

"No seriously, I appreciate you letting me stay here. Clearly my parents place isn't safe and for the first time in the last couple of days, I feel safe. That means the world to me." I said, feeling cliche but trying to be honest with her.

"I wouldn't have it any other way. Try to get some rest." Ivy said, turning and disappearing down the dark hallway, leaving me in the kitchen.

I twisted the cap off of my water bottle and took a large swig, grabbing the pill I had taken from my medicine bottle and tossed it into the back of my throat, choking it down. *Here you go again, trying to hit on someone that clearly isn't into you, can't you find someone who is actually interested? Good grief. She is just trying to be nice, trying to keep you safe. She feels bad for you because of what has happened, she isn't trying to sleep with you.* I thought to myself, trying to talk myself down from making a fool of myself. I knew that if I hit on officer Ivy and she didn't see me that way or wasn't even actually really gay, it wasn't going to go well in my favor and it sure as hell was going to make staying here even more awkward.

I knew that falling for the cop that had offered to protect me probably wasn't the best idea or the smartest idea I had ever had, but it sure wasn't the only bad idea I had ever had. It certainly wouldn't be my last. I was the queen of poor decisions, my life up to this point, being the perfect example of what not to do and who not to be.

I also was never one to listen to anyone's advice, even my own. I might know what the right thing is to do, or what I should do, but I almost always did the complete opposite. I was smart, extremely smart, but that didn't mean I used my intelligence for the right things, the important things in life.

You need to go to sleep, you have got to get some rest. I kept telling myself over and over, trying to work up the courage to walk down the hallway and get in bed. *But fuck my arm hurts and every time I close my eyes, it feels like I am back in the woods all over again.* I thought, dreading sleep, dreading having to actually lay down. *Stop being a damn pussy.* I shouted at myself internally. Setting my water bottle down on the counter, pushing my medicine bottle across the corner to the middle of the island, deciding that I needed to go lay down, before I lost the courage to do so.

I walked down the hallway, looking out of the wall of windows in Ivy's apartment, looking down at the street, the empty road streaming through the middle of the town. Everyone else was at home, in their warm and safe beds, not a care in the world haunting them. I wanted to be one of them. I wanted life to go back to what it was before I left the bar. I wanted to talk to my best friend.

I wanted nothing more than to just be able to hug my parents again, to go to work like every other boring adult and go to a coffee shop without feeling like I was being watched. I wanted life to go back to easy, to carefree, but I knew that wasn't possible. I couldn't rewind the clock, I couldn't change what was happening around me. It was going to chase me, whether I liked it or not.

I hope Sophie is okay. I need to call her in the morning, fill her in about everything that's been going on. I know I told myself I couldn't get her involved, but I need my best friend. I need to hear her voice. Hopefully she answers me this time.

She is going to lose her mind when she hears what has been happening. I am sure she is still pissed at me for not kissing her back and leaving anyway. Ugh, this is what she does when she gets mad at me, she disappears for a day or two and then resurfaces like nothing happened.

I wasn't trying to hurt her feelings, I wasn't trying to make her feel bad, I just don't see her that way and I definitely didn't want to ruin something amazing for a drunken one night stand that we would have both regretted the next day. I thought, pulling my phone out of my shorts, checking my notifications, hoping that maybe I had missed something from her while Ivy and I were eating dinner, but I hadn't.

I kept reminding myself that rambling in my head wasn't going to get me anywhere, I just needed to call her, put the weird vibes in the past and move on.

I wanted nothing more at this moment than to hear her voice, to be able to vent to her about everything that had happened, to tell her how scared I was right now, to tell her about Ivy. She was my best friend, she was always the person I called no matter what it was about. I could share anything and everything with her. I missed her.

If Sophie doesn't stop being stubborn and answer the phone tomorrow, I am gonna kill her. I thought, sitting my phone down on the nightstand in my new temporary bedroom. My body crawling under the comforter on the bed, my legs sliding across the silky satin sheets, sinking into the memory foam mattress beneath me. I could feel my body drifting off to sleep, my eyes getting harder to keep open, my heart rate slowing the more tired I became, my eyes eventually shutting tight.

09

CHAPTER

09

"AHHHH!" I shrieked, my body writhing in pain as I felt the piercing knife cut into my arm, this time deeper, his blade even sharper than before. I could feel my legs flailing, my arms gripping tight against the pillows but I couldn't wake up, I couldn't open my eyes. I was stuck in a trance, paralyzed and frozen. Laying on the cold, wet, mossy ground, his body standing over me, the blade of his knife dripping my own blood onto my stomach.

He was laughing at me, his terrifying and horrific laugh echoing past us and back again. His teeth gleaming in the night sky the more he got off watching me lay there, screaming for help, hoping someone, anyone would hear me. He knew no one could hear me, he knew that we were too far from any other civilization; that he had me where he wanted me.

I kept trying to see his face, trying to figure out what he looked like, but all I could see were his dark green eyes and his teeth the shadows lurking around him, covering everything else. I could feel my body starting to sweat, starting to panic but I couldn't make myself wake up, I had to keep pushing myself to see what his face looked like.

"Hey.. Hey.. Olivia!" Ivy said, tugging on my shoulder blades, standing over the top of me.

"Jesus, fuck!" I shouted, jolting awake, my body lifting up and off of the bed, terrified.

"Hey, Sorry. I wasn't trying to scare you, I just heard you screaming. I wanted to make sure you were okay." Ivy said, backing up and away from me, her hands held up and out in front of her body.

"No, that's okay. I'm glad you woke me up. I was having a nightmare about him again. Can't seem to close my eyes and see anything else." I said, looking over at the nightstand. Ivy's alarm clock illuminated in the dark room. "Good grief, it's 3 am. I am so sorry. I didn't mean to wake you up." I said, putting my feet on the bed in front of me, tucking my legs against my chest, my arms wrapping around the front of my shins.

"Hey, it's all good. I am just glad you are okay. I heard you scream and I couldn't get in here fast enough. Scared me for a second. I was worried that he had found a way to get in…" Ivy said, finally dropping her arms down by her sides, letting herself relax a little now that I was finally awake.

"Do you think I will ever be able to sleep normally?" I asked, closing my eyes and leaning my head down to the top of my knee caps. I couldn't deny that I was starting to become so sleep deprived that my head was constantly throbbing, my eyes felt like someone had taken a crow bar to them.

"Eventually, but probably not until we find him." Ivy said, my head lifting to look at her while she talked. She was fidgeting her hands again, putting them in her pockets this time.

"Wanna sit here?" I asked, sliding over to the middle of the bed, making room for her.

"Are you sure?" Ivy asked, taking a step closer to me.

"Yeah." I whispered, leaning my head back down on my knees. It felt like I was losing my mind and quickly. My life felt like it was starting to crumble, falling apart at the seams, losing control and I couldn't do anything to stop it.

Ivy walked toward the bed, her shorts pulled down slightly on one side, her Woxer brief band exposed. Her cut off t shirt resting slightly above the band, sitting on her abdomen. *Good lord. Her V cuts are showing again and I just asked her to get into bed with me.* I thought, taking a deep breath before Ivy slid into the bed beside me, her legs sliding under the heavy weighted comforter, her hip grazing against mine, her arm brushing up against my forearm.

"Man, I never realized how comfortable this bed is. I got it more for looks than anything else, haven't actually slept in here before, but damn." Ivy said, chuckling as she let her legs slide around the sheets, her legs moving like a hockey puck across ice.

"Yeah, they are pretty fantastic. You have been missing out." I said, laughing at the way she kept sliding her legs back and forth. This was the first time I had seen her do anything that wasn't serious, that was even remotely close to being silly. It was adorable watching her lighten up, watching her be herself for a moment, my eyes darting to her cheeks as her smile lit up the darkened room.

Ivy stopped laughing when she realized I was watching her, her legs slowly stopping in front of her, her eyes peering at me over her shoulder blade. Her smile started to slowly fade as her facial expressions became a little more serious again, her eyes refusing to leave mine, my stomach starting to do somersaults with how intently she was looking at me.

Her face was close enough to mine again that I could feel her breathing against my cheeks, the city lights from the park filtering through the window in her spare room; lighting up parts of her face, exposing her perfectly cut jawline.

I couldn't move, I didn't want to move, I wanted to stay here, letting Ivy protect me for as long as I could, feeling her warmth beside me for as long as she would let me.

"I better go back to my room." Ivy said, her hands dropping down to the bed, beside her legs. I dropped my legs down, letting them lay flat in front of me. Ivy's fingers brushing up against my thighs, her touch sending a jolt of electricity though my legs. *Please don't go.* I thought to myself, wanting to say the words out loud. Wanting nothing more than to beg her to stay with me. I didn't want to be alone, that was the last thing I wanted right now and I felt safe with her, I felt calm when she was close to me. *Ivy, say something. Tits. Stop being a baby.* I thought to myself, trying to muster up the courage to use my voice.

"You don't have to." I said, my voice barely audible. Lower than a whisper, the words leaving my lips, my body in slight shock that I had been able to choke the words out. I hadn't known Ivy long, I really didn't know much about her, but what I did know is that she was a kind soul. She had a heart that ran deeper than any other human I had ever met. She brought me peace when my life felt like it was standing in the pits of hell.

Ivy sat next to me, quiet as could be, the look on her face screaming that she was thinking. Screaming that she had something she wanted to say but she wasn't saying it. I could feel my anxiety starting to grow the longer the silence overtook the room, I had crossed a line, I had taken it too far. I shouldn't have asked Ivy to stay with me. I could feel myself starting to panic, needing to fill the silence in the room. I knew I had to say something, I had to fix the mess I was creating, again.

"If you want to go back to your room, you can, of course. I'm sorry if I shouldn't have said that." I whispered, shifting my body down into the bed, trying to hide my face. I was absolutely mortified, completely embarrassed that I had just asked Ivy to stay with me. I hadn't meant anything sexual about it, I just wanted her to lay beside me. I wanted to be close to her, I wanted her to hold me, to remind me that it would all be okay, somehow.

"I…" Ivy started to speak, stopping herself again, her lack of communication starting to drive me insane. *Just spit it out, spit something out!* I thought, screaming internally to myself as I was pulling the comforter up toward my face, trying to hide that I was squirming inside. I didn't want her to see that I was 2 seconds away from losing it, that my face was probably more red than a stop sign at this point.

"Look, I want to, I really do but I know myself and I don't trust myself." Ivy said, shifting the weight of her body from one hip to another, her body still not moving off of the bed, lingering beside me.

"You don't trust yourself?" I said, letting the comforter drop in front of my face, sitting my body up and turning to face her. "What do you mean?" I asked, the silence in the room making it obvious that Ivy's breathing had started to slow, she was taking deeper breaths, more labored breaths.

"No, I don't, not with you." Ivy said, her hand sliding across the sheets. Her fingers touching my leg even more, her pinky starting to trace against the outside of my thigh. I kept staring at her, watching her chest rise and fall, looking down at her waist, her stomach showing again. I wanted so badly to let my hands roam her body, I wanted so badly to be closer to her, to kiss her.

"Why with me?" I whispered, letting my leg slide closer to her, hoping that she would touch me more, that her hands would get even closer. Her touch felt like electricity jolting my soul alive, awakening something in me that had been in hibernation for too long. I wanted to know why she couldn't trust herself around me, I needed to hear her say it.

Ivy turned her body toward mine, her shoulders facing the front of my body, her eyes maintaining eye contact. "Because, I like you." Ivy said, her face turning the lightest shade of pink, the reflection shining from the window behind me, teasing her cheeks. "But I know this isn't the time or the place. I didn't ask you to stay with me so you would sleep with me. I asked you to stay here so you could feel safe, so I could watch over you, so I could protect you." Ivy said, fully turning her body toward mine.

"I'm not in the business of taking advantage of women when they are in compromised positions, when they are vulnerable, might run in my blood, but I refuse to be that way." Ivy said, her face becoming even more serious the longer she talked to me.

"I get it. But just so you know, I like you too and I didn't think you were taking advantage. For what it's worth, you do make me feel protected." I said, turning toward her, our bodies finally fully facing one another, her legs criss-crossed in the shape of a butterfly, my body sitting similarly. "Among other things…" I said, whispering under my breath, partially hoping she would hear me and partially hoping that she wouldn't notice. My emotions felt like they were riding on a rollercoaster, going up and down, never knowing which direction they would go next.

"Want some company sleeping?" Ivy asked, her hand sliding across my calf, tracing my skin, leaving goosebumps in a trail where her fingers had been. I looked up, smiling, a sense of relief overcoming my body, a deep breath releasing from my chest. "Yes, yes I would love some." I said, twisting my body around so that I was facing the window in the room. Ivy following behind me, her body laying close to mine, her hand sliding across the top of my tricep, her fingers dancing.

I slid into the covers, letting my head sink into the pillows, pushing my body further back, closer to her, her body so close I could feel the heat radiating from her. I was both in shock that she had said she liked me and unsure of where to go from here, my life was slowly starting to fall apart, spontaneously combusting into flames.

I knew this wasn't the most ideal time to develop feelings for someone, much less having it be the person who saved my life and then let me stay with her but I wanted her. I wanted to know more about her, her life story, what made her happy, what made her sad.

I wanted to see the Ivy that she hid behind closed doors. I wanted to know what lied deeper in her soul than what she let others see on the surface.

Ivy stretched her arm, letting it slide from the top of my hip, under my arm and around my waist, her body closing the gap between us, her waist resting against the small of my back, her fingers gripping tight against my stomach. I felt my heart start beating crazy fast again, my breathing staggered, caught off guard in the best way possible, her breath against my neck, her lips grazing the outside of my ear, "And just so you know, you make me feel things too." Ivy said, her voice making my stomach flip flop back and forth, doing back flips deep in the base of my belly.

I felt my eyes jolt open, my mouth opening the second I realized what she had just said to me, she had heard me. I cleared my throat subtly, trying to hide the fact that she had gotten my attention. My teeth teasing my bottom lip, nibbling, my tongue grazing my lip, my thoughts threatening to cross lines I knew they shouldn't.

I looked up, letting my eyes wander to the window across the room, hoping to focus on something besides my labored breathing and pulsating limbs. My eyes catching the reflection of Ivy, watching me from behind, her eyes staring through my soul. *You're caught.* I thought, darting my eyes back toward the bed, pressing my body further into her, my hands grabbing her arm and pulling it closer to me, the strength in her arms, both reassuring and extremely arousing. I needed to close my eyes and try to go to sleep before I made a decision I would regret, before I lost control of my body, my mind. The longer I laid next to her, awake, the chances of me trying something were escalating and at a rapid pace. The chemistry I felt with Ivy was unlike any other chemistry I had ever had with anyone, it was powerful and dominating. It was becoming an addiction and quickly.

CHAPTER 10

I opened my eyes, the sun beaming into my room, my body stretched across the bed, relieved that I had finally gotten some genuine sleep. I pushed my body back, noticing that Ivy's arm was no longer wrapped around my body, the cool sheets hitting my skin. I flipped around, realizing that there was no one in bed beside me, the room completely silent, my door closed.

I let my hand wander across the sheets where Ivy had been laying, her imprint still in the pillow she had laid down on, the fresh citrusy wood undertone smell of her cologne lingering on the sheets. I laid there, remembering the night before, wishing that I could go back and have the courage to kiss her, that I wouldn't have chickened out, but relishing in the fact that the way she held me made me feel at home.

What time is it anyway? I thought, moving Ivy's pillow out of the way, the alarm clock shining across from me. *10:32, holy shit I died in my sleep.*

I sat up, wiping the sleep from my eyes, letting my body stretch. Releasing the tension that had been building in my muscles, realizing that my arm wasn't throbbing near as much as it had the day before. *Finally, I can move my arm without it feeling like someone is holding a match to my skin. Thank God... I wonder where Ivy went?* I questioned myself, realizing that I needed to get out of bed, that Ivy probably thought I was one of the laziest human beings she had ever met. I hadn't slept in until 10:30 since I was in high school, even the times when I was sicker than a dog and didn't want to get out of bed, I was always awake and ready to go by 9 at the very latest.

Clearly I needed the rest. I thought, trying to give myself a little credit, trying to be gentle on myself, something that I wasn't used to doing but with everything that had happened over the last few days, it felt necessary.

I hopped out of bed, stopping by the mirror Ivy had hanging on the wall, redoing my hair and putting it back into a less messy, mom bun. I changed my shirt and threw on some comfy sweat pants, slipping my feet into my slipper moccasins. I wasn't the most feminine woman in the world but I wasn't exactly a tomboy either. I was somewhere in between, but when I wanted to be comfy, I resonated more with an over exhausted pigeon than anything else.

Well, if she still finds me attractive after this, then maybe there is a chance. I giggled to myself, realizing that I looked about as attractive as a sloth right now. *One of these days Olivia, you are going to get your life together, one day, just not today. Ready?* I asked myself, looking back at my reflection in the mirror, slightly terrified to walk down the hallway, worried about how Ivy was going to react after last night.

I opened the door to her spare room and walked down the hallway, peering into her bedroom, the door was open but Ivy wasn't in her room. The light in her gym was on and the radio was lightly playing Lauren Sanderson's music on repeat, her weights scattered across the bright red yoga mat on her floor but again, I didn't see her. *She has amazing music taste.* I thought as I continued down the hall.

    I kept walking, trying to figure out where Ivy was, her kitchen was completely spotless again. My water bottle missing from the night before, the dining room tidied up, each chair placed back perfectly against the table. The rest of Ivy's apartment was silent, the only audible sound was the lingering sound from the radio in her gym room.

    I turned past the dining room, peeking my head into the living room, hoping that I would see her somewhere, that she hadn't left me here all alone, but there was no one. I kept walking circles around her apartment, starting to feel panicked, starting to worry that I was by myself, a sitting duck for the psycho maniac chasing after me.

    I felt my breathing change again for the thousandth time over the last few days, my mind trying to stop racing, my heart fluttering and skipping beats. I could feel my anxiety starting to escalate, the fear of being alone creeping up behind me, threatening to take me down.

    I didn't want to feel this way, I didn't want to be scared to be alone, but until we found him, until he was caught, it felt like I was going to lose my mind anytime I had to be alone.

I scurried toward the front entry way, looking at the cut out in the wall where she had thrown her key card the night before, realizing that her keys and her key card were both gone. *She left, she told me she wouldn't leave me alone without telling me.* I thought, panic full fledge eating at me, my nerves on edge, my heart rate starting to race, my anxiety escalating. I felt my knees buckle, my body falling to the floor, curling myself into the fetal position. I wasn't coping, I wasn't dealing with anything I was feeling and life was starting to suck the air straight out of my lungs. It was starting to rip me apart piece by piece.

Tears started streaming down my face. I felt like a little kid lost in the store. I felt like a crazy person. Like I was losing my mind, but I couldn't handle this anymore. I couldn't handle feeling like he was going to kill me every time I turned around.

I heard the door push open, the bottom of the door hitting my foot, my body lying on the floor, panic riddled and immovable. I closed my eyes, hoping it was him, hoping that he had found me, that he had kept his promise, that he would make this nightmare stop.

"Woah, what happened?" Ivy said, tossing her keys into the cut out of the entry way and dropping a paper sac full of groceries on the floor, apples rolling every which direction across her floors. She dropped down beside me, concern written all over her face, her hands sliding across my cheeks, pulling me toward her, forcing me to look at her.

"Are you okay?!" Ivy shrieked, higher pitched than I had ever heard her before, her voice shaking. I couldn't speak. I was still shaking, still bawling my eyes out, still panicking internally.

All I could see was his body standing over me in the woods still flashing in and out of my thoughts. I couldn't shake the thought of him finding me, I couldn't shake the feeling that he would know when I was alone and he would come for me. I knew I was acting like a small child right now, that I was acting out of character, but I couldn't stop it. It felt like I was watching a train wreck in slow motion. It felt like I was in the train, barreling straight toward a gap in the track, begging to fall off, begging to fall to my death.

"I'm so sorry. This is mortifying. I am so sorry." I said, trying to turn my face. Ivy's hands refusing to let me, gripping my face tightly but also in the most gentle way. She pulled me close to her, letting my face rest against her chest, my tears soiling the front of her shirt, her arms wrapping around my body, being careful not to press against my arm too tightly.

"Talk to me." Ivy said, her hand moving to my hair, pressing gently against the side of my head, trying to console me, trying to calm me down.

"I woke up and realized you weren't in bed anymore. I came out and looked for you and couldn't find you..." I said, realizing that I was starting to sound like a complete sociopath. "I just, I freaked out. I freaked out that I was alone. I'm so sorry. You shouldn't have to deal with this, it isn't your mess to clean up." I said, pulling away from Ivy, trying to turn my body around so she couldn't see my face which I was sure was splotchy and rough at this point.

"I want to be there for you. Stop saying sorry Olivia. You have been through a lot and until we find him, it isn't going to stop. Please don't apologize for being human." Ivy said, twisting my body to where I had no choice but to look at her. Her face leaning toward me, her forehead pressing gently against mine, her hands sliding back across my cheeks, her fingers sliding into the bottom part of my messy bun, "I just placed a delivery order for groceries. I don't like telling them what apartment I live in so I meet them in the garage. I never left you. I promise." Ivy said, her nose brushing against mine.

"Even if you had left, it's okay. You aren't my keeper. This isn't what you signed up for. I don't know how to deal with this. I don't know how to make it stop, his body standing over me keeps flashing into my mind, the feeling I had that night, it refuses to go away. I guess I need to call my therapist." I said, starting to sob again, holding on by a thread. "It makes me wish he had just finished me off, that I didn't have to deal with this; the aftermath, him chasing me, taunting me. Maybe I would have been better off dead, maybe the girls who didn't make it, maybe they were the lucky ones." I said, realizing how selfish I sounded, realizing that I was being immature and that I needed to just stop talking.

"Don't say that. You are the lucky one, the only one, so far, at least that we know of. I for one, am glad that you made it out, that you beat him. We are going to beat him, he will not win." Ivy said, her jaw clenching as she pulled me back into her chest, her fingers tracing the back of my arm.

"I just need it to stop. I have to find a way to think of something else, I can't do this right now. I need a damn distraction." I said, pulling away from Ivy, lingering in front of her face, her eyes making contact with mine, her cheeks still rosy red from being in the cold seconds before. I let my hand graze her lips, forgetting for a moment, that I shouldn't be touching her.

Ivy leaned forward, my fingers dropping from her lips, her nose grazing mine. Her lips gently pressed against mine, reluctant at first. Her lips pulling back slightly, looking at me, wanting to make sure that she had consent, my eyes refusing to leave her. I slid my fingers across her cheeks this time, letting my fingers intertwine in her hair, gently tugging, my thumbs pressing into her cheekbones, pulling her closer to me, begging her to kiss me again.

Ivy let her lips press against mine again, her breathing speeding up slightly, her tongue teasing my bottom lip, dancing along the edge, her hand gravitating toward my waist, sliding under the bottom of my shirt. Pulling me closer into her, my head tilting back, my lips pulling away from hers, teasing her, wanting her to chase me, wanting her to show me how badly she wanted me.

"Jesus." Ivy whispered, her lips finding mine again, her teeth dragging along the bottom of my lip, sucking, little whimpers slipping from her throat. "Okay, okay… I need a break." Ivy said, pulling away, her hands still lingering on my hips. "Wow." Ivy exhaled, her breathing still labored. Standing up, she reached for my hands and helped me up off of the floor.

I stepped closer to her, "You all right?" I asked, relieved that I could finally ask her the same question she had been asking me over and over the last few days.

"No, I need a cold shower after that." Ivy said, pulling the edge of her shirt down over the spandex of her Woxer's, hiding the rainbow colored text on the waistband, covering her hips. She leaned down, picking up the apples that had scattered all across her floor moments before, putting them in the top of the grocery sack, trying to distract herself.

"Maybe later." I said, winking at her as she stood up, the grocery bag in her arms. Her forearm muscles tensed up, her face in shock at what I had just said. I turned around and walked into the kitchen. "Want some help putting that stuff away?" I asked, trying to change the subject, my thoughts finally merging to another topic, one that was a lot more appealing, but almost as frightening. I wanted Ivy and I wanted her bad. My mind still hanging out in the gutter, lingering in the most dirty place I had ever let it go. She turned me on, and fast. She made my mind go to places that I hadn't ever let it go before, I liked it but it was also terrifying.

"Sure…" Ivy said, slowly walking behind me, following me into the kitchen. Ivy sat the bag of groceries down on the counter, unloading everything piece by piece, her mind still in other places. "I got a little bit of everything. I didn't know what you liked or what your preferences are, so I tried to just get the general things that we would need for now until we can go to an actual store."

"I appreciate you doing that. Seriously. I can cash app or venmo you, if you want me to. I figured we would need a few things with me staying here." I said, playing with my bottom lip, still thinking about the way Ivy's lips felt on mine. Thankful for something else to focus on, needing something to cloud my thoughts and keep me preoccupied.

"Don't worry about that. Keep your money, you might need it for something else. Have you decided what you want to do about work?" Ivy said, emptying the last of the grocery bag onto the counter, sitting produce bags side by side. "If you want to just stay here, tell your boss you need the time off, you are welcome to. Money isn't an issue for me, I don't mind helping if that would make you feel safer... Or, if you want to go back to work, I can talk to chief and have someone come with you, make sure that you are okay."

"I have no idea yet, to be honest. My boss isn't expecting me for the next couple of days. I am supposed to let him know something by Sunday." I said, grabbing an apple from the counter and slipping it under the faucet of her sink, letting the water drip down the sides of it.

"I don't want you to do anything you don't want to do. Whichever decision you make, I will help in anyway I can." Ivy said, throwing the bag in her recycling bin. Ivy stopped for a second, her eyes filling with sadness, "Olivia, I know you don't want to think about it, but when we are done putting this stuff up, do you want to try and sit down, maybe see if we can piece anything together?"

"Yeah, we can." I said, realizing that no matter how much I wanted to forget him, that I wanted to act like that night never happened, it wasn't realistic, and it wasn't conducive to finding him. I could spend all day making out with Ivy, forgetting that he even existed, but I knew that wasn't practical.

Bzzz.Bzzzz.Bzzzzz. Ivy's phone started vibrating on the counter, the screen of her telephone lighting up. She sat down the jug of tea in her hands, picking up her phone, looking at the name across the screen and whispered, "I'll be right back."

Ivy walked down the hallway stopping right before her bedroom door, her voice carrying down the hall, echoing across the walls. "Shit." I heard her say, her voice changing and fast. She sounded concerned, she sounded panicked. "When did that happen?" I heard her say, her voice getting lower, less audible.

I walked around the island, her voice becoming more distant, my footprints barely making a sound. I was tip toeing as lightly as I could. I didn't want her to know I was listening, but something was going on, something that didn't sound good. "Okay, and you are sure?" I heard Ivy say, her voice starting to crack a little as she asked the question. I could feel my nerves starting to build back up, realizing that whatever was going on, more than likely was about him.

"Okay. I'll tell her and I'll be at work tomorrow. She is going to stay at my apartment over the weekend, can you send another officer to man my parking garage while I'm working?" Ivy said, her voice ringing across the hall way again. I stopped right where the wall met the hall, my reflection beaming back at me against the

131

wall of glass in her loft. *Shit, shit, shit.* I thought, realizing that if she turned around at any second she would be able to see me, standing there, spying on her.

I turned around, walking back into the kitchen, trying to figure out where the last couple of items she had bought went, acting like I hadn't heard a word, trying to seem like I was clueless to her phone conversation.

"Everything okay?" I asked, looking up at Ivy as she rounded the corner, her face sheet white again. A look of fear hiding behind her eyes. It was bad, there were no doubts in my mind.

"Olivia, I need you to sit down." Ivy said, forcing her phone into her pocket, her chest inhaling a deep breath before exhaling again, her face shouting that something was terribly wrong.

CHAPTER 11

I walked over to Ivy's living room, finding a spot on the couch, curling my legs under my body. I had no idea what she was getting ready to tell me but I felt like I could vomit. I felt like I was going to pass out waiting on her to finally speak up and say something.

"Please tell me it isn't about my parents." I said, wincing. Even at just the thought that something bad had happened to them.

"No, your parents are fine, as far as I know. That's not why the chief called me." Ivy said, sitting down on the coffee table so she was facing me, her elbows resting on her knees; her hands cupping each other into a ball.

"Okay, well if it isn't about my parents, then what is going on." I said, still reeling for answers, needing to know, wishing Ivy would just spit it out already before I lost my shit.

"It's Sophie." Ivy said, the words burning like fire as they rolled out of her mouth. My stomach felt like it was dropping into my toes, my heart stopping, the world coming to a halt.

"What… about…. Sophie?!" I spat, barely able to get the words to come out; processing what she had just said to me.

"They found her in her house. Someone called in a wellness check because they hadn't heard from her since the night you all went out. One of our police officers found her... She's gone." Ivy whispered, choking on her own words.

Ivy didn't even know Sophie, she had never met her, but she knew she was my best friend. I had told her how much I cared about her. She knew that this was going to break my heart and I could sense she didn't want to say the words, she didn't want to have to break the news to me.

"No. No. No. This cannot be happening. No. It's not true." I said, standing up off of the couch, screaming, shrieking, each word stabbing at the back of my throat as it flew from my mouth.

"No, there is no way. Sophie is perfectly fine. She was just ignoring me because she was mad at me. They have to have the wrong girl. They have to be at the wrong house." I screamed, in complete and utter shock. My body going completely numb, my legs buckling and my body falling back onto the couch.

"NO!" I wailed, tears starting to roll down my cheeks in droves, my breathing suffocating. It felt like someone had stabbed me in the chest, like I had a knife sticking straight into my back.

"Ivy, it can't be Sophie!" I yelled, still refusing to believe what I had just heard her say.

"I am so sorry Olivia. I am so sorry." Ivy said, trying to decide what to say to me, what she could say to me. There was nothing she could say. Nothing that could change how I was feeling right now. Nothing that could make this okay, that could bring my friend back.

"What. Happened. To. Her?!" I snarled, clenching my jaw, anger building in the pit of my stomach, hostility starting to surface. I knew. I knew in the back of my head that it was that prick. That sinister demon had done something to my best friend.

"Chief didn't give me a lot of details, I think he knew I would tell you..." Ivy said, my eyes filling with more and more tears, everything in the room starting to blur. I felt Ivy's hand touch mine, her fingers gently resting against mine.

"Tell me what you do know. Please." I whispered, unsure that I even wanted to know, but needed to know.

"He stabbed her. But he didn't leave a note behind like he did at your parents house, which means it might not be the same person." Ivy said, grimacing, clenching her teeth tightly together, "Can you tell me what she was wearing when she went to sleep the night he chased you?"

"Why?" I asked, my head jolting up, my eyes shooting daggers towards Ivy. "Why do you need to know that?"

"They found her in bed, wearing pajamas, like she had been asleep." Ivy whispered, "Chief wanted me to ask you what she was wearing the last time you saw her so we can figure out a time line. She had been laying there... for a little while before they... found her." Ivy said, tripping over her words, trying to articulate what needed to be asked and said, without sounding like a callous and heartless police officer.

"Before I left her house I helped her change into one of her black night gowns. It was the easiest thing to get on her since she was so drunk, all I had to do was slip it over her head...." I said, thinking back to that night, waiting for Ivy to tell me if that's what they found her in, my throat closing tight, the air in my lungs burning each time I took a breath.

"Okay." Ivy said, standing up, "I need to call chief. I will be right back." She said, standing up and walking into the kitchen.

I was in complete shock, my world was quite literally falling down around me, one by one everything I loved was being torn apart, chewed up and spit back out at my face. People I loved were being taunted, terrorized, and now murdered.

I am going to fucking murder this piece of shit when I find him, I don't care if I die trying! I screamed inside of my head, dropping my face into the palm of my hands, my sobs continuing, refusing to stop.

I left her alone, I left her alone to die. I am the reason she is dead, I am the reason he came back for her. He couldn't have me so he took something I loved instead. And I didn't even take the time to check on her.

I was so worried about my own damn life that I let my best friend die because of me!

My mind was spiraling, each thought getting a little more grim as they came and went. The world was starting to feel like a dark place, a terrifying world that I didn't want to live in anymore.

Ivy started to walk back over to me, dropping her phone to her side, clicking the button until the screen shut off, her phone falling into her pocket. She looked like she had seen a ghost, her face was stoic, somber.

"He fucking went back to her after he escaped? DIDN'T HE??" I screamed, losing control of my emotions, letting my anger take control, letting my rage take the driver seat.

"We aren't sure. But we do know that they found her in a black nightgown." Ivy whispered.

"I can't do this anymore. I cannot fucking do this anymore Ivy. I will not let this man take everyone I know and love and throw them in the trash like they don't matter. I won't let him do this. He can have me, he can have what he really wants instead of destroying the rest of my life and all of the people in it!" I said, standing up, my body shaking uncontrollably. I wasn't going to stand there and let him take out everyone I knew one by one until he found me. If he wanted me, he could have me. I was really who he was after, I wasn't sure why or what I had done to him, but clearly it was bad enough that I deserved what was coming to me.

"I'm going to my parents house. If he is watching me, he will come." I said, standing up and off of the couch, hurling my body towards the kitchen and down the hallway, Ivy chasing behind me.

"NO, you aren't. Olivia, you have to stop for a second. I know this is a lot, but you have to be smarter than him. You can't let him, or whoever it is, win. They aren't worth it." Ivy said, grabbing the back of my pants, her fingers locking around the stretchy band, trying to get me to slow down.

I stopped turning toward her, screaming, "This is a lot, Ivy? My best friend is dead and it's MY fault. Whatever this prick wants, he can have it, clearly this is personal, clearly this is about me. I don't even give a shit anymore. She was all I had, she was the only real friend that gave two damns about me, Ivy! Wonder why he didn't leave a note, wasn't this supposed to be some SICK game he wanted to play? Why not go ahead and leave me another bread crumb, really dig that knife deeper into my soul!"

I flung the spare bedroom door open, grabbing my bag from the floor and tossing it onto the bed. Rifling through it, I looked for something to change into.

I finally found a hoodie and some ripped jeans after fumbling through my bag, my hands refusing to work.

"Olivia, stop." Ivy said, gently putting her hand on my forearm. "I know you want to kill him. I want to kill him, honestly. But you can't just aimlessly chase after him, he will kill you. I don't know what he wants with you. I don't know why he is so obsessed with you. I don't know who he is. I really don't even know anything about him, but I do know that you are worth more than this guy. We might even be dealing with two different people, as fucked up as that sounds. We don't have enough information yet but your life is valuable and I don't want you to get hurt. Please, just give me the rest of the day to see what information I can get. I promise, we will find whoever did this, whoever was chasing you." Ivy said, her hand sliding up my arm, pulling me toward her.

I felt my entire body cave against her chest, I had been trying to stand up straight. Trying to keep myself together, but I couldn't do it anymore, I felt like my world was collapsing and I was going with it. Ivy pulled me close, holding me against her body, keeping me upright, her arms wrapped tightly around me.

"I'm so sorry about Sophie. I know she meant the world to you." Ivy whispered sincerely, her voice faltering as the words left her lips. "I promise, I will find them and when I do, they will pay."

CHAPTER 12

The next few hours felt like a complete blur, a blip in time itself. It felt like I was living in the twilight zone. Watching my life burn down from the outside looking in. I couldn't seem to wrap my head around the fact that this was real life, that this was my life now.

Ivy had finally persuaded me to stop trying to leave, reminding me that if I died, that didn't mean he was going to go away. That whoever they were, were going to leave the rest of my family and friends alone. It just meant that I wouldn't be there to help stop him anymore. He would be free to keep doing as he pleased; wreaking havoc on my life and everyone else's.

"Hey, I know today has been horrible. I know you have a lot on your mind and there really isn't a good time for this, but I think maybe we should sit down and see if we can piece together what we know." Ivy said, walking from the kitchen into the living room.

I hadn't spoken hardly a word since she had conned me into sitting on the couch, the tv playing in the background, my eyes glazed over, my mind disassociating from reality. I had seen her walking in and out of the room, periodically checking on me, but for the most part she had tried to give me the space she thought I needed.

"Okay." I said, out of words, completely at a loss. "You do this more than I do, what do you want to know? I feel like I have told you most of what I can remember, but I will tell you whatever you think might help." I said, feeling defeated, trampled on.

"Well, let me go get a notebook. I'll ask you a few questions, see what we can come up with. I have to go back to work tomorrow, so whatever we come up with, I'll relay to chief. Maybe he will have something from Sophie's house that we can use to tie this all together." Ivy said, turning toward the industrial metal book shelf that was mounted on the wall beside her tv. Her fingers pulling a journal out of a stack of books.

"Hold on, I found a journal but I need a pen." Ivy said, jogging across the room to her kitchen junk drawer, fishing around until she found something to write with,

"Found something." Ivy said, walking back into the living room.

"Okay, I know you told me everything you could remember about that night already. Let's start somewhere else, somewhere we haven't talked about yet." Ivy said, pulling the strap off of her black leather journal, bending the front cover back, exposing the cream colored paper inside.

"Okay, what do you want to know?" I asked, looking up at her, finally breaking the trance I had been locked in. My eyes burning from the tears I had shed and the lack of blinking over the last few hours.

"Well, do you have any enemies, that you know of? Someone that would "blame" you for something?"

Ivy asked, my mind trying to sort through years of existence. Turning pages that I hadn't opened in years.

"Uhm... I really don't know. I guess I would have to think about that." I said, realizing that even though I was only in my 30s, I had lived quite a long life. I had come in contact with all walks of life, going through many stages of growth, changing friends, lovers, everything. How was I ever going to be able to pick apart my life, peeling the layers back enough to think of one person, or even a group of people that would hate me enough to kill my best friend and to try to kill me and my parents?

"Ivy, I really have no idea. I'm sure I have hurt people over the years, but enough to motivate them to do this?" I said, realizing that no sane human being could have done any of this. That the person we were dealing with, had something seriously wrong with them. "And the guy at the bar, the creepy asshole that kept staring at me, he didn't look familiar at all. I mean, know I was drunk, but I feel like if I had known him, it would have stood out to me." I said, still trying to figure out how all of these pieces could fit together, how I could make it all make sense.

"And don't forget, he knows you too. He knew you were a lesbian. Unless you have a billboard ad somewhere that you go around flashing, he has to know who you are too." I said, realizing that neither of us had ever discussed that fact. That we had brushed over it for the most part. Focusing on everything else important that had happened. My mind started to dig deeper, hoping I would find something in my accordion of memories that was growing every second the hands on the clock behind us changed.

"Okay, let's go back to his notes, I took photos of them with my phone." Ivy said, pulling her iPhone out of her pocket and opening her gallery, swiping through a few photos and then stopping.

"In his first note he says, 'You might have gotten away this time, but it won't happen again. Go ahead and stay with that little lesbian cop, she can't save you. You deserve each other. Thieves mingle with Thieves.' And in his second note that he left upstairs he says, 'Olivia, want to play a game…? In the hospital you wanted to know how I knew your name, oh, but you are the one to blame. Memories will come and memories will go, my presence will never leave you though…'" Ivy said, reading from both photos, the words striking a nerve, rebuilding the fire in my soul that I had worked hard to put out.

"Let's start with the first note he left." Ivy said, re-reading what he had written, pacing back and forth, mumbling the words out loud over and over.

I sat on the couch, trying to process what he had written. Finally allowing myself to really think about it. I had avoided his notes, hoping that the police station would have something by now, that I wouldn't have to be doing this. I had never coped well, even as an adult. I was the type to avoid things, to not make a decision at all, letting life make decisions for me. I was good at finding distractions, things to keep me from having to feel, from having to accept that my heart felt anything.

The first part of his note was easy. It was a message to me, that I might have gotten free, but the next time he came after me, he was going to do everything he could to make sure it was the last time he chased me. The second part though, that's where things started to get a little more unclear and a lot more confusing. He knew Ivy was a lesbian, even before I realized that she was a lesbian. In my mind that screamed that he knew her, that he had information on her, something possibly from the inside.

We deserve each other. Thieves mingle with Thieves. What in the hell does that even mean. He was right about Ivy being a lesbian. That he wasn't wrong about, but I haven't ever stolen anything in my entire life and Ivy is a cop, I don't exactly see her being a thief. I thought to myself, the puzzle pieces weren't making sense, I felt like we had most of the pieces, but there were a few very important pieces missing.

"Ivy, I haven't ever stolen anything in my entire life. I haven't been a stand up person. I have done some horrible shit in my life… But stealing is not something that I ever picked up." I said, still confused, lost. "And, you are a cop, I know that not all cops are good people, but you don't exactly scream, thief." I said, looking up at her, hoping she could give me some sort of insight.

"No, I mean, I don't steal. Never have. I'm human. I have made mistakes, cop or not, but I'm no thief. I might have stolen a pack of gum when I was little from the grocery store, but that's about all." Ivy said, chewing on the end of her pen, her thoughts lost in the notes.

Ugh. I have no idea what he is even trying to say. It doesn't make sense. Maybe he thinks I am someone else? I don't know. Okay, what did his second note say? I thought, trying to remember what the last note said. *In the hospital you wanted to know how I knew your name, oh, but you are the one to blame. Memories will come and memories will go, my presence will never leave you though… I am the one to blame for him knowing my name… Memories come and memories go, my presence will never leave you though.. He obviously thinks he knows me.*

"Ivy, I still have no idea who this could be, but from both of his notes, the only thing I can come up with is that he knows me, he knows us. I can't come up with anything else, both are cryptic, but they both point toward this being someone we both know." I said, realizing that I really didn't know that much about Ivy. I didn't know who her friends were, I didn't know if she was from here, I had no idea what her life had been like or if she had enemies.

147

"Ivy, this has all been about me, but since he knows you too, maybe we have a tie somehow?" I asked, hoping that I was onto something, that I had found a clue that could help.

"I mean, he knows I am gay and he knows I am a cop. He didn't really say much else about me though." Ivy said, still chewing on the end of the pen, pacing back and forth from the kitchen and then back into the living room.

"He also said he knew I would be staying with you. How did he know that?" I said, a light bulb inside of my head instantly switching on. We had only talked about that one place. Ivy stopped dead in her tracks. Her feet coming to a complete halt, the pen sitting at the edge of her teeth, her eyes looking up at me and stopping instantly. She pulled the end of her pen out of her mouth, closing her lips, the words in her mind refusing to spill.

"Ivy, the only place we talked about me staying with you before he could have written that note, was at the hospital." I said, an overwhelming feeling taking over my body, the same feeling I had felt when I realized he had been in my parents house, the feeling of being watched, of being violated.

"Olivia, you are right." Ivy said, refusing to say another word, her body language screaming uneasiness. "I'm gonna make a call. I'll be back. Keep thinking. Good job." Ivy said, walking off and down her hallway, this time, all the way into her room and shutting the door behind her.

I sat there for a minute, realizing that I needed to write all of this down. I needed to see if I could find a timeline, if I could place things into a more organized manner than just speaking out loud. My brain was scrambled, complete mush and I felt like the more I talked about everything that had happened and was going on, the more confusing things were getting.

Maybe if I write this all down, create a solid time frame of when things happened, I can find something, missing pieces, anything. I wonder if Ivy has another notebook. I thought, standing up and walking over to the book shelf by her tv. I hadn't spent much time looking around her apartment. I didn't want to invade her privacy and I hadn't really had much time to inspect anything even if I wanted to anyway.

She has to be one of the most OCD and organized people I have ever met. She has her books in alphabetical order and there isn't a speck of dust anywhere in her house. My bookshelf is starting to look like it's growing a wig at this point. I thought, slightly embarrassed that I wasn't more like an actual adult at times. *Well, I don't see a notebook, but she has a lot of books, that's for sure. Hold on, that might be a notebook.* I thought, seeing another leather bound book that looked similar to the one she had pulled out to write on earlier.

I pulled it from the shelf, trying to make sure I didn't disrupt any of the other books. Her books were lined in a perfect row. I opened the front of the leather book, a legal pad attached to the back side. *Perfect.* I thought, turning toward the kitchen to find the junk drawer she had just gotten a pen from. A stack of photos started falling to the floor from the inside sleeve that was attached to the front cover of her journal. The photos flung across the floor, darting in every direction, scattering.

Shit. Shit. Shit. I thought, mumbling the words out loud as well, my body scurrying to pick each of the photos up off of the floor before Ivy came back out of her room.

I gathered all of the photos into a pile and shoved them on top of the leather binder and walked over to the kitchen, laying it open flat against the island counter top. I had to hurry or Ivy was going to think I was snooping through her stuff, which was not what I wanted at all. That wasn't what I had been trying to do in the first place. I was just looking for something to write on. *Great, how does this kind of thing always happen to me.* I groaned internally, stopping at one of the photos.

That guy looks familiar. Who is he? I thought, recognizing the mustache and similar facial features. *That's the chief, with Ivy, but she is a little girl in this photo.* I thought, looking at the picture, realizing that the chief of police was next to Ivy at her 7th birthday party. Posing with her, hugging her in front of a giant number 7 balloon. *Wow, they have known each other for a long time I guess.* I thought, holding the photo in between my thumb and pointer finger.

"Hey, whatcha looking at?" Ivy said, startling me, my fingers dropping the photo. I had been paying so much attention to the picture I found that I didn't even realize Ivy had come out of her room.

"Oh, I didn't mean to find these. I was looking for a notebook like the one you had a minute ago so I could make a timeline of events and found this one. When I opened it, these photos fell on the floor. Sorry." I said, slightly self-conscious and hyper aware that I probably looked like an invasive and nosey person.

"No, that's okay. Which photo is that?" Ivy said, walking around the other side of the island toward me, her eyes making contact with the photo, a smile covering her cheeks.

"Oh, I remember that day. It was a big day for me, 7th birthday and the Chief adopted me." Ivy said, still grinning, her eyes distracted, thinking back to her childhood.

"Oh." I said, a little caught off guard. "The chief is your dad?"

"Well, sort of. He is my step father. My real dad abandoned me when I was about 4. Ran off with one of his mistresses and made a new family. Left us behind for New York." Ivy said, nonchalantly.

"Until about a year ago, he only called about twice a year when he lets me know that he has deposited money into my trust. Other than that, he is just a sperm donor." Ivy said, her face changing expressions to one I hadn't seen before. I wasn't sure if it was sadness, anger or maybe even a combination of both.

"Until a year ago?" I asked, hoping I wasn't prying too deep into her personal life.

"Yeah, I keep telling my sperm donor I don't want his money but he doesn't listen. Keeps putting it in there so he can feel a little less guilty, I guess. Lately he has been calling more and more, threatening to show up here even though I have told him countless times I don't want him or his money. At this point he refuses to stop sending it so I use it to pay for this place and save the money I make." Ivy said, tucking the photos back into the leather binder. "Chief is my father. He may not be blood, but he is the man who raised me. I owe him everything."

"Wow. I am really sorry about your real dad. That's terrible…" I said, really not sure what to say. "I am glad that the Chief was there for you though, I can tell you really respect him, must be a good man."

"He is. He has always made sure I had what I needed and more. He has gone to hell and back for me.

He is the reason I work at the station in the first place. I wanted to make him proud. I wanted to be like him. I wanted to help people." Ivy said, thrusting her body onto the counter.

"Well, my dad didn't leave like yours, he stayed. But for a long time, I wasn't sure that he was going to." I said, my voice turning to a light whisper.

"It's a long story but my parents started fighting around the time that my brother started acting out. He had always been a hyperactive kid, pretty disobedient and quite a handful at times. As he got older, it just kept getting worse. I found alcohol and drugs in his closet, just a bunch of stuff. My parents started fighting non stop about him and some other guy that my dad thought my mom was cheating on him with." I said, looking across the room, my eyes looking through the wall of windows, watching the people walking downtown. "I really don't think my mom was cheating, I think she was just tired of fighting with my dad over my brother, but it almost tore them apart for good. My mom is too worried about what people think of her to cheat, at least, that's how it feels…"

"Anyway, my parents couldn't agree on anything when it came to my brother regardless of if there was another man. It almost tore them apart… My brother ended up moving out when he was 16, left us all behind without so much as a word. I was at a Summer Camp when he left, came home and he was gone, every single trace of him. Even with all of his problems, I loved him, wanted nothing but the best for him, looked up to him. Sure, I told on him to my parents from time to time when I knew he was doing stuff he shouldn't because I was worried about him, concerned for him. I was only 13 when he left, broke my heart, felt like my best friend had abandoned me. I thought we had been close but he left me high and dry." I said, Ivy looking at me, listening intently.

"Wow. Do you talk to your brother at all now?" Ivy asked.

"No. I haven't heard from him since he left. For a long time I was devastated... Even tried finding him once I reached adulthood but it was like he disappeared in the wind. My parents stopped talking about him. Removing most of his photos from the wall except for a few in our upstairs hallway... They were hurt. Really hurt that he could just up and run off. They tried to find him for a while too but it was pointless, he was gone... I guess at this point all I can hope is that he is alive and okay somewhere in the world. Hell, maybe he is living it up on a beach in Mexico right now, better than the nightmare I am living right now. Maybe he is the lucky one." I said, trying not to let myself get emotional again.

"I don't really know why I told you that story, other than, I just wanted you to know that I get it. It hurts when your family leaves, makes you feel like it's your fault somehow, like you are to blame for them not wanting to be around." I said, walking over to Ivy, her legs dangling from the counter, my hand resting against her thigh, my body leaning across the island.

"So, anything from that call you had to make earlier?" I asked, trying to change the subject. Hoping that I hadn't crossed any lines with her. It was nice to hear small stories about her life, nice to get to know her a little, especially since we were living together right now, but I didn't want to push, make her open up to me about things she didn't want to talk about.

"Well, I called Chief. Wanted to tell him what you came up with, he is going to send some officers up to the hospital. See if they have any security footage, talk to the nurses and staff, see if anyone saw anything at all out of the ordinary." Ivy said, her thigh moving closer to my hand, pressing against the side of my thumb, my thumb tracing her skin. "I really just want to make sure there isn't anyway he could have snuck into your room while you were sleeping. As creepy as that may sound, it makes sense. When I came to see you, you didn't move. You were completely out of it and you didn't even remember me coming by the first time. As much as I don't want to say this out loud, he could have easily come into your room or been lingering in the hallway and no one would have known."

"I think that's a good idea. It really freaks me out to think he could have been there, that he could have been watching me somehow." I said, trying to vent but not wanting to feel anything anymore. Annoyed that while we all had our thoughts about what could be happening, nothing felt concrete, nothing felt certain anymore.

"Yeah, when you said that, it hit me hard. I don't know why I didn't think about that earlier. Clearly I am a little too involved in this." Ivy whispered.

"Well, too involved or not, I am glad to be here." I said, looking up at her. "If I wasn't here, I would probably be dead by now."

"I won't let that happen." Ivy said, her eyes piercing mine, her jaw clenching and tensing up almost immediately.

"Olivia, I have to tell you something." Ivy said, her jaw clenching even tighter. "That's not all Chief and I talked about on the phone."

"What now?" I asked, backing away from her, turning my body so I could see her directly. I couldn't handle anymore bad news, I was already one step away from the ledge, threatening to nosedive over.

"Some of the results came back from the forensics lab." Ivy whispered, her voice starting to crack a little. "The blood on the door handles was linked to a match."

CHAPTER 13

I stopped. Standing dead still, my body in a trance. I couldn't speak. I didn't want to ask. I wanted to know, but I didn't at the same time. My heart felt like it could explode all over her perfect flat.

"Who was the match? Was it his blood?" I asked, scared, nervous and so much more.

"It was Sophie's." Ivy whispered, tears instantly starting to form in my eyes again as the words slipped from her lips.

"I fucking knew it! I knew he was the one who had done this to her!" I shrieked, the words hitting my chest like a bag of bricks, crushing my lungs. "Jesus! This guy is a pure psychopath…"

"I think we need to sit down and make that timeline now." Ivy said, jumping off of the counter, her feet hitting the ground. The setting sun peering through the window, almost peaking behind the trees. It was starting to get dark outside, a time that I used to love, that I used to crave. A time that I now hated, that reminded me of all of the evil in the world.

"Yeah." I said, choking back my tears, trying to swallow my anger and sadness. I was tired of this man making me feel this way. I was sick of letting him control me, letting him manipulate me, letting him play this sick and twisted game. "Come on." I said, walking to the other side of the island, grabbing the notebook and pen I had found.

I walked over to the dining room, turning the fireplace on as I walked by.

"Is it okay that I turned that on? It's a little cold." I said, my body shivering, goosebumps appearing everywhere, realizing that I hadn't ever even changed out of my pajamas from the night before.

"Of course. That's what is there for." Ivy said, sitting down next to me at the table.

"Okay, let's start from the beginning."

Ivy and I worked on the timeline for hours, rehashing everything that we knew. Writing each detail down in chronological order, making sure we didn't leave anything out, the puzzle pieces slowly starting to fit together.

"So... basically if it's the same guy from the bar, the staring asshole. He followed me and my friends to their houses after we left. I got to Sophie's and helped her inside, helped her change while he was standing outside of her house. Waiting for me to come out. I came out onto the porch and saw him and that's when he started following me which led to him chasing me to the woods, that's when you showed up and he took off..." I said, looking at the timeline we had just created, making sure we hadn't left anything out.

"Then, after he escaped the other cops he rounded back to Sophie's at some point...." I said, refusing to utter the words, refusing to acknowledge that she was really dead. "And then I am assuming at some point he went to my parents house, looking for them or me and got pissed when he realized neither they or I were there."

"I just don't know where the hospital fits into all of this. I didn't get to talk to you the night you were admitted, they wouldn't let me. I came back the next morning and that's when we talked, but I didn't offer for you to stay with me until later that night after I had talked to Chief." Ivy said, still trying to figure out how he could have heard us, where he could have been. "If they wouldn't let me in your room, I don't know why they would let someone else come see you, unless he snuck in somehow. I really wish we already had the security footage from the hospital already." Ivy said, the hair on the back of my neck starting to raise.

"Well, I don't put anything past this man. I would tell Chief when they get the security footage to check out everyone, including the staff, make sure he didn't find a way to disguise himself. I've seen in movies where the killer dresses up as a staff member to escape past security…" I said, shivering at the thought of him watching me, staring over me while I was unconscious.

"Yeah, that's a good idea. You sure you don't want to be a police officer? You seem like you would be pretty good at this job." Ivy said, chuckling a little, the mood lightening for a moment.

"I used to do investigative reporting for the New York Times actually. My job was to find out things that no one else could, dig up dirt on people, find skeletons in people's closets." I said, letting my inflated ego shine for a moment even though I hated how that job made me feel. I hated feeling like everyone relied on me to find dirt on people. I was thankful that life had turned upside down for me in a way, allowing me to find something, calmer.

"Olivia, that could be something!" Ivy said, her eyes flashing toward mine.

"What do you mean?" I asked, confused by what she had just said.

"I mean, what if it's someone you uncovered something on? What if you found out something about them that they didn't want you knowing and now they blame you for it? Coming after you for revenge?" Ivy said, her teeth starting to chew on the inside of her lip. *She must get that from Chief, he does it too when he is stressed and thinking. Watched him do it in my parents kitchen.* I thought, eyeing her as she chewed even harder.

"I mean, I guess, maybe it could be related to that. Most of the stories I wrote about, the people ended up getting locked up in prison." I said.

"That doesn't mean people stay in prison forever Olivia. Can you think of anyone at all that would have gotten a lessor sentence, someone that could have lost everything? Someone that thinks you stole from them?" Ivy whispered, jotting a few things down on the notebook in front of us.

I started thinking, realizing that maybe there was a link, maybe that would make sense.

If I had found out something about someone and they weren't happy about it, they could want to make me pay for ruining their lives, dragging out their hidden demons. I knew the job could be dangerous, I had put myself into plenty of horrible positions, scary moments when I thought something bad could happen, but never anything like this, never anything that would lead to murder.

"I mean it makes sense. I guess it never occurred to me that someone could be that big of a psychopath, that they would hold a grudge for that long. I can try and think back, maybe see if anyone sticks a chord. But then what does he mean when he says, 'You deserve each other. Thieves mingle with Thieves.' How do you play into this if it's someone I pissed off in New York? And not only that, if this guy is the same person that had already been killing people before I ever came in contact with him, then I doubt he is someone from New York." I said, all of the different parts of this starting to fry my brain. It felt like there were so many different things happening at once and I couldn't make them all fit. There had to be more to the story than we knew.

"That part, I don't know. We still don't know if the murders over the last year have anything to do with this or if they are unrelated. Just mind boggling that Cartlon, of all places could have two people going on a killing spree at the same time. And you are right, if it's someone from New York…I don't know how I have a part in this at all except for you staying with me and me being a cop. You and I didn't even go to school together, right?" Ivy said, realizing that neither of us had even talked about school or whether we could have mutual friends.

"I graduated in 2010. What about you?" I asked.

"Oh yeah, no, we didn't go to school with the same people. I graduated in 2003, I'm 39." Ivy said, giggling. "Quite the cradle robber it seems." She said, winking at me, biting her bottom lip, her tongue teasing it. *Whew. If this man doesn't kill me first, the way she looks at me will.* I thought, trying to catch my breath, trying to hide how she made me feel.

I knew this wasn't the time to try and get into the hot cops pants, even if that's what I wanted. Even if it would help me forget everything going on for a little bit, even if I was craving a distraction, from her.

"6 years isn't cradle robbing, thank you. Makes it sound like I'm a child." I said, bantering with Ivy, trying to appreciate the little moments when I could forget the reality around us. "Believe me, I can feel every bit of 33, it's not fun. Every joint in my body started popping and snapping the day I turned 30." I said, chuckling.

"Oh I understand that. I hit 30 and instantly felt 10 years older. Now that I am almost 40, I regret hating my 30s." Ivy said, laughing.

"Enjoy your 30s while you still can. Once they are gone, the pops and cracks you feel now, will start to feel like someone beat you with a baseball bat. I swear it takes me 10 minutes just to stand up in the morning, my back screams at me, constantly."

"Well, you don't look almost 40, at all. I would have never guessed, to be honest. You hide it…very well." I said, looking down at the table, peeking up at Ivy, my cheeks flushing pink.

"Getting hot?" Ivy asked, my eyes darting toward her. *How did she mean that?* I thought, realizing I didn't know how to respond.

"What do you mean?" I croaked.

"Your cheeks, they are flushed. And the base of your neck is turning pink too." Ivy said, grinning at me.

"Oh yeah, it's probably just because I turned the fireplace on… It's getting warm in here." I said, trying to hide the fact that she was the reason my face and neck were starting to burn alive.

"Here, I can turn it off. Want to put a pause on all of this? I think we have done enough for one night." Ivy said, closing the notebooks we had been jotting information down in and shoving them across the table.

"I don't know about you but my brain feels a little fried right now. It's been a long day."

"It's been the never ending day. Feels like we have lived a lifetime in one day to be honest. A break, would be nice…" I said, standing up and pushing my chair back in. "A distraction, would be even better." I whispered, walking toward the hallway, avoiding Ivy as she stopped and looked at me.

That one, I hope she heard. And I hope she knew exactly what I meant. I thought, biting my lip and walking down the hallway. Secretly hoping she would follow me, that she could be my distraction.

My therapist would absolutely have an issue with this, she would tell me that using sex as a distraction was exceptionally unhealthy. She would lecture me saying it wasn't going to solve anything and it could possibly ruin a friendship or whatever Ivy and I had going on, but I really didn't care. My coping skills hadn't exactly been up to par my entire life and I wasn't going to attempt to fix that now. At this moment, I really didn't care what my therapist would think, if I was going to die, I wanted to at least die happy.

I kept walking down the hallway, purposely taking my shirt off while I was still in the middle of the hallway. Hoping that Ivy would be watching me, from wherever she was, that she would enjoy her view. That it would strike something in her, remind her of the way we both felt during that kiss.

I dropped my shirt to the floor, right inside of the spare bedroom. The small of my back arching as I stretched my arms above my body, my ass bending backwards. I wanted to turn around. I wanted to know if she was watching me. I wanted to know if she wanted me the way I wanted her.

I lingered there for a second, looking through the window in my new room, watching the leaves on the trees sway back and forth, taking in the colors of each leaf, all of them different autumn colors. It was honestly breathtaking even at night. The view from Ivy's spare bedroom faced the edge of a park, the landscape perfectly manicured, the trees peaking above the grass, the city street lights and the lights from a distant apartment complex, illuminating the entire park.

I stood there finally realizing that Ivy wasn't going to come down the hallway, even if she had seen me, she was too good of a human to take advantage of my situation. She wouldn't dare just come into my room if she knew I was changing, that I would be naked. She was too chivalrous for that, too respectful.

I appreciated how old school she was, that she knew how to be polite and courteous. Something that most people nowadays had no idea how to do.

And while I loved that she didn't want to cross a line with me, that she was trying to give me space and be a fantastic human. I wanted nothing more than for her to just come to my room and make me hers.

Why does it have to be her that makes the first real move? You've already kissed her and it was amazing, unbelievable, to be honest… Stop being a scared little bitch, Olivia. I told myself, trying to work up the courage to go find Ivy.

Just because Ivy is more tomboy, less feminine, doesn't mean she has to be the one who goes after what she wants. You can do that too. You should do that. Stop fearing what's behind closed doors and do something that scares you for once.

"All you have to do is find Ivy and just kiss her, what's the worst thing that could happen." I said, whispering to myself out loud.

I finally gathered enough nerve, mustering up enough courage that I turned around to go find Ivy. Except, Ivy was already standing just outside of my doorway. Her arms above her head, resting on the door frame, the muscles in her arm flexed and bulging.

"The worst thing that's going to happen is… I kiss you back." Ivy said, staring at me with desire.

CHAPTER 14

How long has she been standing there? I gulped internally. Refusing to blink, refusing to take my eyes off of her.

"That's the worst thing that's going to happen?" I asked, hoping she would understand my inference.

"That depends entirely on you." Ivy said, leaning into the door way, her muscles tensing more and more as she leaned further forward. I took a few steps toward her, slowly closing the distance between us, the smirk on her face growing.

Where has this cocky attitude been hiding? I thought, thoroughly enjoying the look she was giving me, shocked that she was even standing in my doorway.

"And why is that?" I whispered, bitting down on my bottom lip, stepping closer to her, our bodies inches apart.

"Because I know what I want." Ivy said with confidence, her eyes looking my body up and down, lingering around my waist and then coming back up slowly to mine. "But just because I want something, doesn't mean, you do too. I'm sorry I didn't knock. I was just coming to check on you before you went to sleep… I didn't know you had already started undressing."

I took one last step, closing the gap between us, reaching my hand up to her exposed arm, letting my finger trace across her muscles and down to the top of her chest, stopping at her shoulder muscles.

"I've been staring at these since the day you came to see me at the hospital." I whispered, leaning my face toward hers, letting my lips almost graze hers and then pulling back from her, grinning and pressing my lips together, her eyes following my lips. "You don't need to be sorry, at all, I was hoping you would see me. If I am being honest…"

I moved my hand down the front of her chest to her stomach, lifting on her shirt, letting it slide up to the bottom of her sports bra, letting her shirt cling to the fabric of her bra, hanging. "And I've been staring at these as well." I whispered, letting my finger graze across the v cuts in her abdomen, my finger sliding underneath the waistband of her sweat pants. Ivy took a deep breath, her arms dropping from the wall to reach for me. My hands reaching for hers and propping her arms back to where they were. "Who said you could move?" I breathed, clenching my jaw and smiling at her.

"Fuck." Ivy whispered, the blood rushing to the base of her neck and migrating up to the bottom of her ears, her cheeks flushing just as red. "Yes ma'am."

I lifted her shirt the rest of the way up and over her head, letting it drop onto the floor next to mine, pushing her arms back up to the sides of the door. I let my hands sliding down her chest again, teasing the outside of her bra, letting my fingers graze across her nipples, making them harden under my fingertips. I looked up, lust filling her eyes, desire written all over her face, my stomach flipping upside down and back around.

Ivy let out a slight whimper as I continued to tease her. My fingers lingering across her skin, dancing across her breasts, tracing down to the top of her pants, tugging on them, letting them drop slightly, the band of her boxers, exposed.

"Let's see just how bad you want it." I said, tilting my head so that my lips touched her ear, my teeth dragging across her earlobe, my tongue tasting, sucking, my breath lingering in her ear.

Ivy dropped her hands, letting them grip around my body, lifting me up and off of the floor, my clit instantly throbbing with desire. "Oh, I'll show you." Ivy breathed seductively. Her body guiding mine to the bed, laying me down, thrusting me backwards across the bed, her body placing itself on top of mine, her lips finding mine.

I pressed my lips against hers. My tongue dancing across her tongue, twirling and teasing her, my teeth pulling on her bottom lip, sucking, little whimpers escaping from her throat. She pushed her knee in-between my legs, letting the top of her knee thrust against the outside of my pants, a moan bursting from my lungs.

Ivy moved her tongue down to my neck, turning my head slightly, letting her tongue glide down the front of my neck to the top of my breasts, her fingers sliding around my back, unclasping my bra, letting it loosen from my body, her other hand ripping it away and tossing it across the room. Ivy gripped the base of my throat gently, her tongue sliding down to my nipples, her mouth enveloping them, sucking and biting, her teeth grazing over the top of them, her knee thrusting into me again, another moan broke free from my lips, desire consuming my entire body. *I want to feel her inside of me, I want to taste her. I just WANT her.* I thought, trying to keep myself from begging.

    I leaned my head back. The small of my back arching up and off of the bed, pressing Ivy's knee in between my legs again, wanting to feel her against me over and over. Ivy moved further down my abdomen, her tongue and lips dragging across my skin, her teeth gently grazing, leaving a trail of goosebumps behind with each touch. She gripped the top of my pants and started tugging on them, letting them fall to my thighs and then ripping them off and letting them fall to the floor, her eyes wandering across my body, her tongue finding its place again, twisting circles across my stomach, right above my thong.

    I lifted up, pulling on my thong, Ivy sitting up to let me get it off. I tossed it across the room with our other clothes and then flipped Ivy around to her back on the bed. "It's my turn." I whispered, tugging on her pants, pulling them and her boxers down until they were off, our bodies naked and exposed, pressed together.

"You are so damn sexy." Ivy whispered, her breathing becoming more labored, her words full of thirst and hunger.

"Likewise…" I said, breathless, my fingers lingering down her body to the top of her thigh, threatening to move up further, teasing her, taunting her.

"Don't make me beg." Ivy whispered into my ear, her lips moving down my neck, her teeth biting down, her body starting to tremor the closer my fingers moved.

"Or what?" I asked, enjoying her groveling, watching her body slowly losing control, her desire growing with each touch.

My fingers grazed the top of her lips, her moans getting louder, her breathing becoming faster as my fingers started to touch her clit.

"Please…" Ivy begged, "I need you inside of me…"

I let my fingers graze her clit, taunting her one last time, enjoying her being vulnerable with me, loving that I could see the need on her face, that I could feel her desire dripping on my fingertips.

I slid two of my fingers in, a loud moan breaking free from her mouth, her back arching and raising from the bed, her feet pressing into the sheets. Ivy slid her hands behind me, letting her nails dig into my back, gripping me tight against her the deeper I touched. I thrusted inside, letting my fingers curl, moving in and out, my body sliding with my hands, our bodies becoming one, sweat starting to drip from our skin.

"Oh. My. God." Ivy screamed, her body losing control, her legs starting to shake beneath my fingertips, my body moving faster, gliding on-top of her, thrusting harder inside of her, her hands reaching down toward my ass, pulling me further into her. I could feel her close in around my fingers, her orgasm building, both of our breathing staggered and labored.

"Holy shi...." Ivy whispered, taking a deep breath, her body lifting up, bending, her orgasm coming to a climax, her voice cracking. Her body going completely limp along the bed.

"Wow." Ivy said, hardly able to get the words out. "I have never had sex like that in my life." She said, our naked bodies tangled together, interwoven as one. I loved the way her body felt against mine, the way she held me tightly against her.

"I can honestly say, that was the best I have ever had as well." I whispered, tucking my face into the crevice of her neck, kissing her lightly, tasting her one last time. "I can't believe it's almost 3 a.m."

"Yeah, tomorrow is going to be rough. Well I guess today that is. But it was so worth it, every single second of it." Ivy whispered, her arms gripping me tighter, avoiding the gash that was still on my arm.

"Oh yeah. I forgot you had to go back to work. I guess the best thing would be for me to just stay here?" I asked, anxiety threatening to emerge.

"If you want, you can come with me. I asked Chief earlier if you could ride with me to the police station instead of having a police officer stay here. He said that was fine. With everything going on, the area of gray with the rules gets a little bigger." Ivy said. "I just want you to feel safe. I don't want you to have to worry. I think my apartment is safe and if we have a patrol car downstairs, no one is getting up here without being noticed. But, I also think you coming with me, would be a good idea too."

"I would rather go with you. I don't think being alone right now would be a good idea." I whispered, my eyes starting to close, comfort washing over me knowing that I could be with Ivy, that she would be there to ensure my safety. I couldn't handle having one more thing happen or I was going to spontaneously combust.

"Perfect." Ivy whispered, her eyes starting to shut, her breathing becoming more shallow. I could lay with her forever, her arms wrapped around me and it would never feel like I had enough time with her. I had never expected anything to happen with us, especially after how we had met, but I was so incredibly thankful that she was here, laying with me, protecting me.

CHAPTER 15

"I am so incredibly tired." I said smirking slyly, taking a sip of the hot liquid bean water at the police station. My eyes lingering to Ivy who was sitting at her desk across from me, hoping she would look up from the stack of paperwork she was rifling through.

"Same, but Chief's tar water should help with that." Ivy said, chuckling, still filtering through the paperwork on her desk, her eyes fixated on what she was reading.

"Yeah, you should probably tell ole' chief that investing in better coffee, maybe some creamer and sugar, might help with employee happiness." I said, giggling. "It would certainly make the patrons here a lot happier."

"Patrons? At a police station?" Ivy asked, snickering. "If you want to call the people who are here patrons, you can. But I can assure you they aren't offered coffee."

"Oh, yeah, I guess that comment didn't make a lot of sense." I said, embarrassed at myself, realizing where we were. Sometimes I didn't say the brightest things, especially when I was sleep deprived and sitting in front of a hot officer, replaying the events from the night before in my head.

"Well, I, as a patron, who isn't here because they did something wrong, think that your Chief, should consider adding other options. This coffee has to be the worst thing I have ever drank in my life." I said, looking down in the cup. Little flakes of coffee beans floating in the top, sticking to the sides of the white styrofoam cup. "However, I believe you are correct about it helping me wake up, there are enough coffee grounds in this cup to put hair on my chest."

"Jesus, please don't grow hair on your chest." Ivy said, laughing. I loved her laugh. It was unique, special, something different and unexpected.

"So, what are we going to be doing today?" I asked, sitting my cup down on Ivy's desk, my eyes lingering to the window behind her desk, her apartment gleaming from a distance.

"Well, I have to leave you in here for a little bit while I go to a debriefing meeting. Bending the rules or not, there is no way Chief is going to let you sit in on that. It's about Sophie, you and whoever this ass wipe is." Ivy said, grabbing a folder from the opposite side of her desk, standing up and walking over towards me.

"Oh, well that sucks." I said, wishing that I could participate. Wishing that I had a say so in my own life, but I understood. Business was business and in this case, there were things I really didn't want to know anyway, things I didn't need to see that were going to be in that room. I had endured enough trauma already, I really didn't need anymore. I couldn't bare the thought of seeing Sophie, knowing everything that had happened to her. I was still in complete shock that this was even real life, that Sophie was really gone, that I had no way to bring my best friend back.

"I know it does. I wish you could be in there. You have found more pieces to the puzzle than even we have. I think you being in there could be helpful but I also don't think it would be good for you either. I should only be gone for about an hour. If you want to sit in here you are more than welcome, no one should bother you." Ivy said, leaning down, kissing the top of my head, taking a deep breath and exhaling loudly. "We are going to figure this out."

"Ok. I'll be here... I am going to try and call Sophie's parents. I couldn't make myself do it yesterday, but I need to. She was my best friend, I can't keep avoiding them, I have to face reality." I said, regretfully.

"If you need me, ill be in the conference room across the hall. Just text me." Ivy said before walking out of the door, clasping it shut behind her, my eyes closing.

I sat there for a moment, anxiety building in my chest. I knew I needed to make this phone call. I knew I needed to talk to Sophie's parents, but I was scared. I knew I was going to be emotional. I knew that I was going to lose it, and I didn't want to do either of those things. I was sick of feeling like my heart was being ripped out of my chest but Sophie had been my person, the only person I could ever rely on when things got hard. She was who I had shared everything with and I owed it to her and her family to be there, in whatever way I could be, to assure them that they weren't alone.

"Hello, Mrs. White?" I uttered, silence on the other line, waiting to hear Sophie's mom's voice. "Mrs. White, can you hear me?" I repeated again.

Silence.

I looked down at my phone, the call had been answered, the time was ticking away and it wasn't ringing anymore. I put the phone back up to my ear and that's when I heard his voice.

"Well hello Mrs. Olivia Sanchez. I've been waiting on your call. Took you long enough. Was starting to think you were even more selfish than I thought." He said, his voice ringing in my ears, piercing my heart like a thousand knives. I felt my limbs lose feeling again, every hair on my body standing straight up, my stomach in knots.

"Why. The. Fuck. Do. You. Have. Mrs. White's. Phone?!" I snarled, standing up and looking out of the glass window in Ivy's office, scanning the other offices across the hall, looking for the conference door.

"We will get to that later. What's important at this very moment is for you to know that both Mrs. White and Mr. White are still alive, for now. But they won't stay that way for long if you don't play my game and play it well." His voice echoed through the phone.

"What do you want from me?" I shouted, losing my cool.

"Hey, hey! I think it would be a good idea for you to lower your voice. If anyone hears you, the White's are done for... Do you understand me? And don't even think about saying something to that lady cop of yours, you know... the one you slept with last night like a whore." He said, his voice getting louder, more irate and unsettled, my heart rate escalating as I realized he had been watching us. "One hell of a way to mourn your friends death." He spat.

"Guess you couldn't bare the thought of staying at her apartment alone, huh? Had to go with her to work, like a little child. You always were hanging on the coat tails of others, don't know why that would change now." The man's voice echoed on the other line.

"What are you even talking about? How do you know what I was doing last night? Who are you?" I said, getting more and more angry, my rage building, threatening to explode. I wasn't going to defend my actions. I wasn't going to let him know that he was getting to me. I was determined he wouldn't be able to sense that I was inches from bursting into tears.

"It's not about who I am, it's about who I was forced to be. But, you will find out who I am with time. What I want from you right now is more important. I need for you to listen to me and listen to me well, one misstep and you can add another one of your precious friends to the list of lives you have ruined." He snarled back at me.

"What do you want me to do? Do NOT hurt them." I said, realizing that I was at his mercy, that I had no other choice but to listen to what he wanted, at least for now. While I didn't want to acknowledge his threats, I wanted nothing to do with him, I knew I had no choice. He had backed me into a corner, once again.

"I want for you to go and find your little lady lover and her fake *fatherrr* once we get off of the phone and I want you to tell them that they have 24 hours, 24 hours only, or the White's will be dead as well. They can bring me both, YOU and *yourrr* parents. And I want both of them there as well." He snapped.

"What do my parents have to do with this?" I said, looking through the blinds on the window attached to Ivy's office door. Trying to decide if I could walk out of Ivy's office without him hearing me, hoping that I could find a way to get her attention.

"Oh, in due time, it will all be very clear." He said, starting to laugh, his sinister chuckle stabbing me in the ears. I started to turn the door handle, trying to be as quiet as I could. I knew I needed to get the phone to Ivy before something bad happened, before I did something that would screw this all up.

I wasn't good under pressure and it felt like my life was imploding from the inside out. One false move and I was going to detonate a bomb around us all.

"STOP!" His voice screamed, a shrill shriek blaring through the phone, a familiar woman's voice in the background, shouting for him to calm down.

"Stop what?!" I said, pulling the door open.

"If you open that door, they are dead." He said, his voice writhing with anger. "I can see you. I see everything you do. You can't hide from me. I've been watching you my whole life and I won't stop, until yours is over. Now, I will repeat myself one last time, DO NOT OPEN that door."

I stopped. Realizing that while I had no idea where he was or how he could see me, he wasn't playing around. I pushed the door shut, letting the latch clasp again, loud enough for him to hear and turned around, letting my vision dart out of Ivy's window behind her desk. I scanned the entire area, looking from one corner of the street to the other, realizing that there were plenty of places he could be, shops and apartments that he could be hiding in.

"What have I done to make you so angry, to make you hate me this much? I don't even know who you are." I shrieked, starting to unravel, frantically trying to figure out who I could have pissed off this much.

"Don't bother asking questions now. You didn't seem to care to ask before, don't know why you would care now… probably because you're selfish. Only giving a shit when it matters for you. When it can benefit your life somehow. Typical Olivia. Just like the all of the other people in this godforsaken town." He said, the woman's voice in the background getting angrier, more pronounced. *I swear to God I know that voice from somewhere, but WHERE?!* I thought, trying to scour the depths of my mind, to remember where I had heard her voice from.

"I'll be at 14117 panther cove paradise tomorrow at 10am sharp. If you, your parents, and the wannabe father/daughter combo aren't there on time… go ahead and bring an ambulance and body bags, because you will need them." He said, the call dropping. My knees instantly starting to feel weak, my heart beating so hard it felt like it was going to lurch from my chest.

I have to find Ivy, now. I have to tell her about this. Conference meeting or not. Shit, this is about what they are meeting over anyway… I thought to myself, holding my phone tightly in my hands.

I turned around and ran to her door, slinging it open, the door slamming up against the brick wall, the blinds shaking so hard they were threatening to fall down. I stopped, my eyes darting around the room, reading every label on each door until I finally found the one for the conference room. The door was shut, the blinds pulled closed, but I could hear voices echoing from across the room.

I ran across the room, all of the other police officers and office staff staring at me like I was a mad woman. My face telling them all the story, there was something deathly wrong and I needed to get it out before I forgot something important.

I ran up to the door, yanking on the door handle, struggling to get the door open, my hands and mind refusing to work together for a moment. I stopped and took a deep breath and then pulled the door handle down again, opening the door open and letting it fling open like Ivy's office door. Every officer and detective in the room instantly jumping and turning around to look at me. I stood there for a second, Ivy and the Chief making eye contact with me, their faces shocked that I was standing there, the projected image in the background glaring at me from across the room.

Sophie was laying in her bed, her black nightgown saturated in her own blood, her face covered in blood as well. Her body was draped across the bed in the most gruesome manner possible. He had stabbed her over and over.

I instantly felt like I was going to vomit, like the world around me was starting to spin. I needed to sit down, but I didn't have that choice. I had to stop being myself for a second and become someone else, I had to do this for Sophie, for myself and for her parents, who were in grave danger.

"I just talked to him on the phone!" I screamed, finally finding my voice, finally letting the words slip from my tongue, their faces instantly changing from confused to serious.

"You did what?!" Ivy asked, setting down the folder she had been carrying in her hands on the desk in front of her, her body moving across the room toward my direction.

"I called Mrs. White, Sophie's mom. I was trying to check on her after everything and…. He answered the phone." I said, Ivy's eyes locked with mine, in a trance.

CHAPTER 16

"Okay, Olivia, I need you to sit down." Ivy said, grabbing my arm, my legs starting to shake. "You look like you have seen a ghost."

"Yeah, I feel like I have seen one." I said, sitting down in one of the chairs toward the corner of the room by the door.

"You to tell us everything that just happened, as detailed as you can be." Ivy said, sitting down on the desk in front of me, the entire room of officers directing their attention my way, their notebooks ready to absorb whatever information I had for them.

It was overwhelming, both hearing his voice over and over in my head and having everyone in the room continue to stare at me, hovering and towering above me.

I spent the next 30 minutes describing to them what all had been said except the part about Ivy and I having sex. I told them what I had responded and even brought up the woman I could hear in the background. I made sure that I didn't leave anything out, including that he kept commenting on Chief being Ivy's fake father. I made sure that everything was accounted for. I knew that I couldn't make a mistake, that there was absolutely no room for error with this asshole. He was waiting for me to slip, hoping that I would fail and I refused to let him win.

"Ivy, it was weird. I don't know how to explain it to you, but that woman's voice sounded extremely familiar. I know her somehow. I cannot for the life of me figure out where I have heard it before, but I know I have. I have been replaying the events from the night at the bar, trying to figure out if I heard it there or if I knew her from school. Or if she could have been someone I interviewed in New York but I just can't figure it out." I said, feeling like I had failed, again. This was my chance to find something that would help them and I couldn't even remember where I knew her from.

"What if this really is someone that I found the skeletons in their closet and exposed them? If they are mad and coming after me and everyone I love now because of it? I mean, since you said that to me it's been driving me insane, eating my thoughts alive. What if I pissed off the wrong person?" I said, my hands starting to shake with tremors, my mind racing in circles, crashing into each other like waves. "I just don't know how that could have anything to do with you, how could you and Chief be involved in this at all, nothing makes sense anymore!" I shouted, my mental capacity well past its limits. Nothing at all was making any sense.

"Just sit here. I need you to keep thinking, remembering everything you can. I know that can be hard, especially when you feel stressed, but I need you to do what you can. If we know who she is, maybe we can find, him and make it all make sense." Ivy said, tapping my shoulder. "Chief and I are going to step out for a minute. I need to talk to him about all of this, alone."

"Where are you going to be?" I said, starting to panic at the idea of Ivy leaving me. Even though I was in a room full of detectives and police officers, she was the only thing that ever made me feel like I was going to be okay, that life wasn't bursting into flames. I needed to be near her, I needed to know she wasn't going to leave me here alone.

"We are just going to step into the hall for a minute. You said he wants us both there… I am starting to believe he knows us, he knows ALL of us, somehow. Chief and I need to figure out if we can find someone that would be involved with all of us. If there is a pattern, a tie that would wrap this all together." Ivy said.

"But we didn't even go to school together or work together in New York? And until this happened, I had no idea you even existed. Who could we ALL know that would do this?" I said, Ivy's teeth starting to chew on the inside of her lip, gnawing from stress.

"That's what he and I need to figure out. I may not have gone to school with you, but I know a lot of the same people you know. It is a small town and my real dad lives in New York. Maybe he has something to do with this… I really would never have thought my own flesh and blood could do this but people will shock you. You need to call your parents, find out if they can get here in time, please babe." Ivy said, rubbing the side of my shoulder again and walking through the doorway into the hall, the rest of the police officers in the room starting to stare at me again.

I sat there, trying to avoid their stares, hoping that they would all just stop looking at me. Praying that they would focus their attention on someone else, besides me.

Ivy was right, I needed to call my parents but I wasn't going to do it with every one of these police officers gawking.

I finally stood up, realizing that they weren't going to stop glaring at me, that most of them sitting in this office were rookie cops and this was probably their first homicide. I could see the looks on their faces, their nervous but excited energy filling the room, each one of them had almost the same vibe to them.

I turned around. Looking back at the door, staring through the glass window, letting my eyes scan the room until I found Ivy and Chief. They were both standing in the hallway talking. Ivy's hands kept moving up and down. I loved how she talked with her hands, how she put so much passion into whatever she was doing, but right now, I could see that she was stressed. She was worried.

I would give anything to be a fly on the wall, to be able to hear whatever they are saying.

"Chief, that address she gave us, that's the old boys home." Ivy said, putting her hands on her leather belt. "Why is he sending us there?"

"I'm not sure. But as soon as she said that address it struck a chord with me… flashback to the past. I haven't thought about that place in years." Chief said, leaning his shoulder up against the wall, his mustache furrowing, his eyes lost in a puddle of confusion.

"There has to be a correlation. That's to specific of a place to send us for it to mean nothing, for it to not be a clue." Ivy whispered, realizing that Olivia was looking through the glass window of the conference room.

"Yeah… This is either a clue or he chose one of the most remote locations that he could. The boys home is in the middle of nowhere, one of the most secluded areas around here. There are so many trees around those grounds, you can't hear anything for miles. He could just be bating us away from town, trying to get us truly alone. That's basically what he has already done to Olivia once, it seems to be his go to. He wants people by themselves, no witnesses at all. That's exactly what he did to Sophie too." Chief said, shifting his body and pulling himself away from the wall, his body blocking my view of Ivy

"Whoever this guy is, he has been to Carlton before, you can't even find a trace of that place anywhere. When they shut it down, they wiped its history almost clean." Ivy said, the hallway falling almost silent.

"Olivia is supposed to be calling her parents soon to see how fast she can get them back in town and I guess our only option is to show up tomorrow morning. If we don't, he will kill them, if he hasn't already." Ivy whispered again, keeping her face hidden by Chief's towering body.

"Do you think they are still alive? Olivia didn't say a word about hearing them in the background, just that other woman." Ivy said, starting to chew on the inside of her lip again, shifting her weight back and forth from one foot to the other.

"I hope they are. We have to get this guy before he hurts anyone else. This is beyond out of hand. He has flown under our radar for way too long. Regardless of who he is, he has to be stopped." Chief said, his voice starting to shake with anger.

"Chief…" Ivy whispered, leaning, letting the weight of her body completely rest against the railing in the middle of the wall. "You think there is anyway this has to do with Seth?"

"What? Why would this have to do with your real dad?" Chief asked, putting his arms across his chest, the muscles in his arms tensing up.

"Well, it has to be someone we all know, at least that's what I am starting to believe, why else would this guy want us all there? Plus, he honed in on you being my "fake" father…And you know Seth isn't a good guy, he's done plenty of shit to prove that through the years, including when he beat the ever loving hell out of mom." Ivy whispered, looking over Chief's shoulder to make sure no one could hear them. "He has been trying to get me to meet with him. In fact, over the last few months he has become pretty persistent, threatening to show up to the apartment 'he pays for anyway'. I really didn't think much of it before, just thought he was on some power trip, but maybe he is, maybe this is his power trip… Chief?" Ivy whispered, stopping her words, trying to collect her thoughts before saying anything else.

"Yeah?" Chief asked, realizing that Ivy's wheels were turning, waiting for her to say something.

"Didn't you say when you saw Olivia that you thought her mom was one of the women Seth was sleeping with way back in the day? That my mom had caught him with her, too?" Ivy asked, starting to realize that maybe Olivia and her's lives were more tangled than she thought.

"Yeah, I did. Olivia's mom was sleeping with Seth way back when but that was before Olivia was even thought of. You were barely even alive when that happened. I really don't know why that would matter now. Olivia's mom hasn't exactly been known around town to be the most faithful human being alive. I'm surprised that her husband has stayed with her this long, to be honest." Chief said, laughing a little.

"I'm just saying, Seth lives in New York. He cheated on my mom with Olivia's mom, he knows you and I both. He was raised here and I'm sure knows the White's. He also used to donate to the boys home on a regular basis… It might not be him, but I am starting to seriously wonder." Ivy said, internally debating if her father really could be the elusive serial killer.

"It better not be him. I'll see if I can pull any records on him, see if he has been in any trouble recently or if he ever had any charges against him we don't know about. I'm also gonna go pull old cases from boys that had been sent to Panther Cove, maybe something will catch my attention. I need the two of you to see if you can remember anyone who might have been sent to Panther Cove you both knew of, anything. And I really need Olivia to think back to when she worked in New York, see if she can think of anyone that might be mad enough to do this. Let me know what her parents say when she talks to them… And Ivy, be careful. This guy is a lunatic, he is psychotic and just because he said he is going to meet us tomorrow morning, doesn't mean he won't try something tonight. Even if this is your father, we both know he is evil, blood doesn't mean anything sometimes. You two stay together and be safe." Chief said, concern showing in his eyes before he walked around Ivy, leaving her and her spiraling thoughts in the hallway.

"Olivia, let's go." Ivy said, pulling the door of the conference room open.

"Yeah, I need some air." I said, realizing that I had been staring at the image of Sophie's body, unable to break my stares. It didn't even feel real that I was standing here, that any of this was actually happening. It was starting to feel like I needed to be checked into a psych ward, that I had royally lost my mind and created an alternate universe of shit.

"Come on." Ivy said, holding her hand toward mine, my fingers sliding across her hand. I was slightly shocked she was being intimate with me, an entire room of police officers behind us, watching. But here we were and there she was, letting me hold her hand. We walked out of the office, still holding hands. Ivy's fingers wrapped tightly against mine, refusing to let go.

"You okay?" I asked.

"Yeah, just trying to run through old memories. Why?" Ivy asked, her fingers locking closer to mine.

"Well, you have my hand in a death grip... You haven't stopped chewing on the inside of your lip since you walked into the hall with the Chief and your face is screaming that something is bothering you." I said, as we approached her police car.

"Olivia, that address he is sending us to is the old boy's home. Do you know anyone that could have ever been there? When you were reporting, did you ever uncover anything that could tie to that place?" Ivy said, stopping beside me, letting go of my hands and shoving hers into the pockets of her pants.

"The old boy's home? I didn't even know we had one of those. I don't think I ever found anything regarding that, it doesn't ring a bell at all, honestly. Was it like a juvy?" I asked, confused.

"Sort of. It was a place they sent boys who had been in trouble, sometimes it was court ordered, sometimes it wasn't. Sometimes it was boys who didn't have a home at all, like orphans. Boys that couldn't make it in their foster homes, that kind of thing. Did you ever have any guy friends who might fit that?" Ivy asked, turning her body and laying against the side of the car, her back pressing against the passenger side door.

"I mean, kind of. I knew this guy in junior high and high school, his name was Erik. It seemed like he was constantly bouncing from foster home to foster home and then one day, he just stopped coming to school, figured he dropped out or moved away. I wasn't really friends with him, but I knew of him. He was kind of weird to be honest, didn't really run in the same crowd that I did... A lot of my friends made fun of him because he was so different... But I don't know if he was ever at the boys home." I said, flipping through pages in my mind, memories from forever ago, a different lifetime. "I really don't know. I didn't even know the boys home existed. Much less that they sent boys from around here there."

"This guy obviously knows us all somehow, he has made that very clear. Chief is trying to figure out if he can come across any old cases that might give us a clue, someone that would have attended the boys home or helped run it somehow, anyone that could make this all make sense.... I didn't know an Erik personally, but I can tell Chief. Have him look up that name specifically and see if it pulls anything up... He is also going to look up my biological dad, Seth. He lives in New York now, knows a lot of the people in this town. It blows my mind to think that he could be behind this, but at this point, everyone man in this town is a suspect, really." Ivy said, lifting her hands from her pants pockets and letting her face drop into her palms, her fingers rubbing her eyes, trying to wipe the exhaustion away. "I'm gonna be honest, this is one of the hardest cases I have ever been on. I have never had a case get to me like this before. Usually I can deal with the situation, find whoever is guilty and move onto the next one, but this one, has ahold of me."

"Well, you have seen my sleep schedule, which is basically non existent at this point. Clearly, it's affecting me too, so you aren't alone on that one. I will say, if it's your dad, he looks young for his age. This guy didn't look young but no way I would have thought he was over 50. Must run in the gene pool…" I said, turning my body, letting my hips rest on the front of her cop car, my legs propped and crossed in front of me.

"Well, my parents had me when they were only 14, got an early start. My biological dad is only 53." Ivy said, shifting her feet across the ground.

"Oh wow, that was young…." I said, slightly shocked.

"Yeah, both my parents had a wild upbringing." Ivy said, not wanting to talk much more about it.

"So…What exactly are we supposed to do until tomorrow?" I whispered to Ivy, realizing that she looked frustrated.

"Have you called your parents yet?" Ivy asked.

"Yeah, I finally called them while I was waiting on you and Chief in the conference room. I was going to wait because all of those other cops kept staring at me but I knew I needed to get ahold of them sooner rather than later. They will be here waiting at the station at 9 tomorrow morning. I told them to stay in a hotel out of town and just come here so we could all go together." I said, my eyes looking across the street to the shops lining downtown. All of the people walking with their shopping bags, not a care in the world on their shoulders.

"They might not even go. I am gonna talk to Chief about having them stay here while we go but I want to make sure we have eyes on them. They have to eventually come home and the more people we take to the boys home, the worse this could get." Ivy whispered, her words feeling like knives in my ear drums. I knew what she was trying to say. I knew she was trying to tell me that they could be safer at the police station, that if they went something horrific could happen to them.

"I don't want them hurt. Whatever we have to do to keep them safe, that's what we have to do." I said, realizing that she was right, that it wasn't worth risking their lives to give him what he wanted, even if it was a risk to break the rules of his game.

"It's probably best that Chief and I go, alone." Ivy said, her words piercing my heart.

"NO. Absolutely not. I am going. This is about me, he wants me. He has made that very clear. You are not making me stay here at the station with my parents!" I shrieked, frustration building, my anxiety creeping across my chest again.

"Olivia, I couldn't look myself in the face if something happened to you. I want your safety, that's what this is all about. If you go there, you are right, you are what he wants, he blames you for whatever it is he is mad about, you will be his target. That's why I think you should stay here. Let me and Chief go and handle the situation. He is angry with us too but this is what we are trained for and we are not the ones who got away. We aren't the ones his obsession is fixating on." Ivy said, lifting herself off of the police car and turning to look at me.

"No, I said, NO! I mean it. You think he won't know? He knows everything. He has seen everything Ivy. He saw us…" I said, looking down at the ground, tossing the asphalt with my shoes, letting little rocks kick across the pavement.

"What do you mean, he saw us?" Ivy said, stopping, her hands grabbing mine, my eyes finally looking back up to her, my cheeks turning red.

"I mean, on the phone in your office earlier, he said he knew we slept together. I didn't want to say anything in the conference room because your step dad was there, the whole room was full of other officers listening in… But he said he saw us. He knew, Ivy…" I said, my eyes locked with hers. Her skin had turned a pale white, her eyes instantly changed from worried to fear and anger.

"That son of a B…" Ivy said, unable to finish her statement before Chief shouted across the parking lot, "Ivy! Don't leave. I need you and Olivia to come back in here. I think I might know who it is.…"

Ivy and I both stopped and looked at each other for a second. My stomach felt like it was going to shit out of my stomach and into my toes.

I wanted to know who it was but I also was scared to death. The reality that I could be moments away from all of the puzzle pieces coming together finally had my stomach in knots. It felt like time had stopped, like it was standing still once again.

If I knew who he was, I would have to face him. I would have to face the reality that someone who knew me could have done this to my friends and my family.

CHAPTER 17

"I was going through old files, pulling up old cases from boys that had been court ordered to serve a time at the old boys home... There weren't a whole lot of these cases and some of them were even destroyed once the boys reached of age if their parents wanted it to go away, but there were still several on file in our back office." Chief said, shuffling through a stack of dusty folders on his desk.

"All of the files from these cases are on paper. We haven't gotten a chance to put them in the system yet and they are so old, we didn't think there was any rush..."

"Who do you think it could be?" Ivy said, twisting in a chair in Chief's office. The walls covered in old photos of himself at work, receiving various awards and even the same photo of them that Ivy had in her journal sitting on his desk on display. He was proud of her. You could see it in everything he did, on his face, in his heart, that was his daughter, whether anyone else thought it or not.

"I think it's your brother... I don't think it's Seth or someone you investigated in New York." Chief said as he stopped shuffling papers on his desk, the room in the air getting thicker as the seconds passed. Time stood still, my mind on overdrive and paralyzed at the same time.

"My brother?" I said, the words barely audible, pointing at my chest, confused, in complete shock. My brother had never even crossed my mind as a suspect. I hadn't seen him in so long, he had just up and disappeared. There was no way that it could be him.

"Yes… I found a case in our file room that I think you should hear about." Chief said, grabbing the file he had been looking for and putting it up to his face. He leaned down looking for his glasses on his messy paper ridden desk, grabbing them and sliding them across the bridge of his nose. He looked closer at the case, reading and turning through the pages, this time without his nose scrunched up and his eyes squinted.

"Your brother would have been 15, almost 16 at the time I believe… It was the first case that I took on with Ivy. She was fresh out of officer training." Chief said, looking up from the file, his glasses slipping to the end of his nose, his eyes looking through the lenses at both of us. I looked over at Ivy, her face in complete shock.

"Your brother is Scott?" Ivy said, looking back at me, a look of horror across her face.

"Yes, that's my brother…" I said, still bewildered. "But what does my brother have to do with all of this? He ran away a long time ago, I told you that at your apartment."

"Olivia… He didn't run away." Ivy said, looking away from me and looking back to Chief, their eyes making contact almost immediately. "Chief, I didn't realize that was her brother."

"I didn't either. Never crossed my mind, until she mentioned the boys home. I didn't want to say anything until I knew for sure." Chief said, flipping through more pages in my brother's file quickly looking for something.

"Ivy, Chief, what the hell happened to my brother?" I murmured.

"Your parent's sent him to the boys home…" Ivy said, closing her eyes. "It was my first real case. Chief came with me to the hospital that night so I wouldn't mess anything up…When I got there, your brother was in pretty bad condition. He had stolen your parents car and gone to a party here in town. His TOX screens came back hot for both alcohol and drugs…." Ivy said, trailing off her words for a moment.

"When the party was raided he took off, trying to escape the cops so he wouldn't go down for underage drinking and drugs. He had loaded up your friend, Sophie and a couple of other younger girls in the car with him and they sped off. He was going way too fast and ended up running off the road, threw himself through the windshield of the car and could have killed a couple of the girls." Ivy said, looking back at me.

My breathing was more and more shallow the further she went into her story. The words holding my lungs in a pair of vise grips, my heart racing with each word that came from her mouth. I felt betrayed. I felt confused. This was not the story I remembered, this was not the story my parents had told me, this was some alternate universe, a different life than my own.

"Sophie ended up walking home. She was only 15 at the time and was worried her parents would find out. She left him there alone and never called the cops. She left him to possibly die…The other girls, did the same thing. Chief… are the other women that were killed, the same girls in that file?" Ivy said, the worlds starting to collide together, the puzzle pieces starting to make more and more sense.

"That's what I was looking at. Yes, they are." Chief said, his words harrowing across the room.

"Your brother is the serial killer. He killed Sophie and he wants us all dead too. He is trying to come for everyone he blames for stealing his life, I'm assuming. *Thieves mingle with Thieves.*" Ivy said, her words dancing around my head, refusing to soak into my mind.

"This cannot be my brother. My brother would not have done these things. He couldn't have done these things…" I said, the tears starting to stream down my face, dripping from my nose and chin one right after the other, memories of my brother flashing in and out of my mind.

"Why did my parents send him to a boys home?" I shouted, still in complete shock, tears still streaming down my face.

"When I got to the hospital he was in bad shape. Your parents were completely beside themselves over everything he had done. They kept repeating that they had done everything they knew to do and they didn't know what else to try but something with him had to change. Your mom was especially worried about you living around him, seeing his behavior, becoming him, she even said that right in front of him…"

"And then she asked if he could be sent to the boys home instead of the juvenile detention center. Chief and I agreed that we would talk to the judge, see if he would agree to that instead, which he did. Sophie and the other girls got off free of punishment because Sophie's mom and dad are attorneys here in town. Her dad was friends with the judge and shoved everything under a rug…" Ivy said, replaying the events from that night.

"Why would Sophie not tell me about any of this? Why did my parents hide this from me? How is it I never found out?" I asked almost rhetorically. Shock radiating through my body, my legs starting to shake uncontrollably, my entire life was starting to feel like it was one giant lie.

"I'm sure you didn't find out about Sophie and the girls because of her parents. They made sure that nothing was ever said about them being involved, that the world would never know that their daughter was hanging out with the local drug and alcohol addicts, especially at 15. I can't speak for your parents though. I'm sure they were trying to protect you. They told me that you were at a summer camp and they needed the judge to hurry, that they wanted Scott out of the house before you came back home…" Ivy said, turning her face back to the Chief's, their eyes making contact.

"How did I not recognize him though? If it's my brother, then wouldn't I have noticed that?! I didn't know this asshole, at all. He looked nothing like what my brother used to look like." I said, my lips shaking, my voice quivering, sadness and anger overcoming my entire body.

"You were only 13 Olivia.. He was barely 16.. That's been over 20 years… He could look like a completely different human now and you only saw him in the dark. You yourself told me that you couldn't really describe much of him because you never got a good look…" Ivy said, trying to help me understand,. Trying to make me feel better. I had been standing that close to my brother, the murderer and had no idea it was even him.

"What do we do about tomorrow Chief? If it's Scott, he wants us all dead more than likely, even the White's. They are a pawn to get us there but they may not even be alive at this point. He blames us all for everything that went wrong in his life." Ivy said, the words hitting me in the chest all over again. The realization that this was my own flesh and blood. This was my brother, the person I had chased after, the person I had tried to find for so many years.

Chief looked up from his file, his glasses still on the bridge of his nose, his face lost for words.

"We go." I said, breaking the silence, answering for the Chief. "We go, you me and the Chief. My parents stay here, they don't need to be involved in any of this. We hope that the White's are okay and we give him what he wants, me." I said.

"I just don't understand why he wants you so bad, what you did to him to make him think this is all your fault." Ivy whispered, needing to say the words out loud but not wanting to hurt me.

"I don't know, but I guess we are going to find out." I said, standing up and turning toward the door, my hand lingering on the door knob. "If this is in fact my brother, I'm going to kill him before he kills me or anyone else." I said, pulling the door fully open, letting it slam against the wall. My steps getting heavier with each touch to the floor, adrenaline starting to course through my veins. *If Scott is behind this, I am bringing that son of bitch down.*

"Olivia, wait!" Ivy screamed across the parking lot, rifling for her keys in her pocket to the squad car.

"I can't go anywhere without you. My car is at your apartment." I said, in a callous, cold voice, forgetting for a moment that she was on my side.

"Olivia, talk to me." Ivy said, stopping at my car door, pulling it open for me, her body standing behind the door, her hand still holding the lever.

"Let's go get a coffee or go back to the apartment. I don't even care where we go but I need to get away from here for a little bit. Can you do that?" I asked, realizing that she was still supposed to be working.

"Yeah, Chief knows what's going on. I'll text him and ask him to divert calls to someone else. Let's go home, we can change and i'll make you a latte, something better than Chief's dirty bean water?" Ivy said, pushing the door closed and walking around the front of the car to the driver side.

"That okay?" She asked, opening her car door and looking down at me.

"Yeah, that works for me. I'm sorry I don't have much to say right now, I am still in shock. I feel sick. I feel the worst betrayal I have ever felt in my life right now." I said, trying to share my feelings with Ivy, wanting her to know that none of this was her fault, that she wasn't to blame for how I was feeling. But I needed space. I needed to be able to process everything that I had just heard, to work through everything that kept continually falling apart in my life and I couldn't do that if she kept prying.

"Okay." Ivy said, crawling in the seat beside me, turning the car on, and pulling on the gear shift. "Home it is." She whispered, looking at me one last time before backing out of her parking spot, her eyes filled with empathy.

The rest of the car ride was silent, the gentle tune of alternative indie music rattling in the background. The silent whisper of the trees blowing outside gleaming through the window.

I zoned out, refusing to acknowledge any of the beauty from the day. Hoping that the day would become a giant blur, a sweat riddled nightmare that I would wake up from eventually. I was so sick of life twisting and turning every second, throwing punches at me before I could even stand back up. For once I just wanted life to be easy, to not have to feel so hard, so unfair.

"Hey, we are here. Wanna get out?" Ivy said, my eyes finally coming back to life, realizing we were in her parking garage, her squad car turned off and my door was opened, Ivy standing behind it.

"Yeah, sorry. I was just thinking. Didn't realize we were already here." I said, snapping back into reality, my feet dropping out of the car and onto the pavement. "I can't wait to change. These jeans feel like a prison." I chuckled, trying to veer the presumed topic of discussion to something else.

"How do you think I feel?" Ivy said, pointing down at her skin tight police uniform, the arms of her shirt gripping her muscles tightly, her muscles begging to be released. Her uniform was snug against every muscle on her body, clinging to her like I wanted to be, painted across her.

"At least you look sexy in your uniform, I look like I'm semi homeless right now." I said, giggling and pressing the button to the elevator, waiting for it to open, Ivy's body closely behind mine.

"You always look sexy." Ivy whispered, her hands clinging to mine from behind, her fingers slipping into mine, the elevator door opening, welcoming us in.

"Well, I'm glad you think so, I wish that we could have one day where our lives were trying to implode, a day where we could actually go do something fun together." I said, realizing that although we had slept together and had the most amazing sex of my life. We hadn't actually been able to do anything normal adults would do for a date. I didn't know all that much about her but I wanted to know more. I wanted to be able to see what life could be like with her without having to look over our shoulders. What life could be like if we weren't being chased by a homicidal maniac.

"When we fix this situation, you and I will go on whatever dates you want and more." Ivy whispered in my ear, her body pressed against mine, her lips pressing gently on my ear. "When this is over, we can finally be able to be ourselves, without having to feel guilty, without having to worry…"

"Promise?" I said, the elevator doors opening in front of us.

"I Promi….." Ivy whispered, our eyes making contact with the same thing at the exact same time, Ivy's words trailing off, unfinished. We both stood there for a moment, the elevator doors open in front of us, in complete shock.

CHAPTER 18

"Olivia, do you see what I see?" Ivy asked, pulling me closer to her, her body pressing against mine, her arm wrapped around my body, keeping me close to her.

"Yeah. There's... a note on your door." I stuttered.

Ivy walked around me, grabbing my hand and pulling me into the hallway and out of the elevator. "Stay here." She whispered, walking down the hall to her door, pulling the note off and pushing on the door, realizing that it was just cracked and not fully closed. Her hand instantly darting to the top of her gun, gripping it tightly in her hand.

"Come here. He got in." Ivy said, my body flinging toward hers, running until I was next to her body, every ounce of adrenaline in my body starting to course through my veins.

"How did he get in here?" I asked, looking down at the key card electronic screen on the wall of her apartment that looked untouched.

"I have no idea..." Ivy rattled, opening the note and reading, "You can run but you can't hide. I already told you once, my presence will never leave you. Try to cheat my game tomorrow and you will lose. Take this as a last warning for both of you. Also, Ivy, you may think your apartment is invincible, but clearly it's not. Next time, I would suggest hiding things you don't want found, a little better."

"What does that mean? Hide things you don't want found, a little better?" I asked, stepping a little bit away from Ivy so I could see her face, waiting for her to answer me.

"I really have no idea what he is talking about. I have nothing to hide." Ivy said, pushing on the door, letting it open and bump against the wall behind it. She started to walk through the doorway, pulling her gun from her belt. Her gaze was fixed on the room ahead of her, her head turning from one direction to another. She raised her gun in shooting position, ready, prepared for him to pop out at any second, scouring each room one by one, looking behind every door. I could feel my heart racing so fast it felt like it was lodged in the back of my throat, fear propelling itself into my body.

"What if he is hiding?" I whispered, trying to overcome the growing angst that I was feeling deep in the pit of my stomach.

"If he is hiding in this apartment, I will find him. Stay close to me." Ivy whispered, slowing down so I could follow behind her as she rounded the corner from the kitchen down our hallway.

Ivy walked slowly down the hall, one foot in front of the other, the reflection from the wall of glass windows beaming back onto us, the sun shining through, our shadows casted across her floors the further we walked, making my stomach more uneasy than it already was. He had opened both of our room doors, leaving them open, wanting us to know that he had been in our rooms, that he had gone through our stuff.

"Ivy if you have something to hide, it's okay. We barely know each other, it isn't like we have had all that much time to talk about skeletons in our closets." I said, whispering lightly against the back of her neck.

"Seriously Olivia, I have nothing to hide. I don't know what he thinks he found but I am an open book. Whatever it is, I will tell you about it once we know what he 'found'…" Ivy said, walking up to her bedroom door, pushing it fully open, the room looked untouched, perfect and immaculate.

"It doesn't even look like he has been in here." She whispered, looking around, inspecting the bathroom against the far left corner of her room and then circling in front of her bed, which was still perfectly made.

Ivy kept walking, looking in her closet and then walking back around to where I was standing, she had a smirk on her face.

"Well, I don't know if he thinks he found a secret in my closet or not, but I believe that may be what he was talking about." Ivy whispered and then kept walking over by her bedroom door.

I flipped around, looking back at her, "What's in your closet?" I said, curious and confused as to why she was smirking.

"You are welcome to look, if you would like." Ivy said, standing up against her door frame, her gun still pointed towards the ground, her finger sitting on the trigger, waiting, ready.

"Okay…." I said, turning back around and walking over to her closet, a line of clothing glaring back at me. "I don't see anything 'secret' in here." I shouted from the closet, still spinning circles, confused, looking for anything that looked like it could be out of place or abnormal.

"Look in the back corner." Ivy said, her voice shocking the hell out of me, my body jumping instantly, having an out of body experience for a moment.

"Jesus Christ Ivy! You scared the hell out of me!" I said, chuckling a little, turning my body toward the back corner of the closet, walking further until I finally could see what he had found.

"Oh… Well then." I said, as close to speechless as I could be. "Didn't quite expect you to have one of those, but, not exactly something to be embarrassed about." I said, turning back around toward Ivy, my hand sliding up the front of her police uniform, a grin overtaking my face. "Pretty sure most lesbians have a hidden stash, it's just usually in a backpack, not in a gun safe."

"Maybe we can try them out sometime." I whispered, winking at her and walked around her, leaving her in the closet. I could hear Ivy closing the gun cabinet in her bedroom that was housing her 'secret' toys.

"So, why do you keep all of that in your gun safe?" I asked, letting Ivy walk past me out of the bedroom, toward the guest room I had been staying in.

"I didn't exactly think that leaving leather whips and bed straps lying around was the most appropriate way to store them. Plus, it wouldn't all fit in my golden retriever backpack." Ivy said, winking at me and chuckling a little. "Wasn't intending to hide any of it from anyone, just didn't think a complete stranger would be nosing through my closet, either." Ivy said, shifting her attention back to making sure the guest room was clear.

"Makes sense." I said, looking around, inspecting everything, realizing that the only thing that had been moved was my bag. "He went through my bag." I said, emptying the contents onto the bed, sifting through everything, "He took the photo of my parents I had grabbed… but that's all." I said, looking back at Ivy.

"Olivia, as much as I know you don't want this to be your brother, him taking the photo of your parents, pretty much seals the deal for me." Ivy said, walking over to where I was standing.

"Yeah, I guess, it all fits. I just can't believe he would do something like this. He was always crazy but never like this. Never to this extent… I just always thought he was a wild teenager." I said, watching Ivy as she put her gun back into the belt of her pants.

"People will surprise you. Unfortunately, sometimes it feels like you never really know who someone is, until they show you their true colors." Ivy whispered, helping me put all of my stuff back into my bag.

"Yeah, I guess, I just hoped that he had found a good place, that he had run away to be better. I never imagined this is where he would end up...." I said, zipping my bag up and then looking at Ivy, her beautiful eyes gleaming and twinkling as the light from the windows shone through. "Even worse, he blames me somehow. I chased after him for years, I looked for him non stop. I never wanted anything but the best for him...." I said, Ivy's hands reaching for mine, her fingers intertwining with mine.

"Sometimes, it doesn't matter what we do, it's about the other person, how they see the world, how their version of reality changed them..." Ivy whispered.

"Yeah, I guess he sees our past much differently than I do. Clearly..." I said, shaking my head, "I'm still in shock. And even worse, he was standing right over the top of me and I had no idea it was him, that he was to blame for this. That this was my own flesh and blood."

"He might be flesh and blood but you aren't anything like him. This isn't your fault, this has nothing to do with you... This is about him and him only. He has created this nightmare." Ivy said, pulling her hands away from mine and walking toward the doorway of the guest room. "Let's change our clothes and get out of here. We aren't staying here tonight, not after this, not without knowing how he got in here." Ivy said, disappearing into the room beside mine.

I changed my clothes as fast as I could, sliding into some comfortable Nike Joggers and my favorite cozy long sleeve Nixon shirt, slipping on my all white vans and then grabbing my bag from the bed.

"I'm ready whenever you are..." I shouted from the hallway, Ivy's door standing wide open, her room seemingly empty, a few clothes draped across her bed. "I went ahead and grabbed my backpack, just in case."

"Okay, perfect. I'll be right out." Ivy shouted from her main suite bathroom. "You can come in and sit down if you want to, I won't be long. Just wanted to wash my face and put my hair in a pony tail before we leave."

I walked into her bedroom, looking around, realizing that apart from when we first got here earlier, I had not been in her room before. The door was almost always closed. I scanned the room looking at the photos of Ivy and Chief throughout the years, photos of Ivy with her friends, even a photo of Ivy from when she played soccer at her university.

Good lord. How can one human being be so incredibly hot, all the time, no matter what they are wearing.... I thought, turning around and looking toward the opposite side of the room, my eyes making contact with Ivy standing between the door of her bathroom and her bedroom, staring at me... *or what they are not wearing...* I thought, taking a small gulp, letting my saliva run down the back of my throat, trying to keep my cheeks and neck from flashing bright red again.

"Sorry, my clothes, they are behind you on the bed." Ivy said, looking past me, her clothes still draped across her comforter.

"Oh yeah, might need those." I said, giggling and turning around, "Here, I'll get them for you."

"Thanks." Ivy said, watching me as I gathered up her stuff, awkwardly trying to hurry, nervously handing them to her.

"You... Are very welcome." I said, looking Ivy's body up and down, looking at the way her perfect breasts were sitting in her bra, the way her body naturally curved in the most perfect ways, her hip bones perfectly sitting against her boxers.

"Can I have them though?" Ivy said, chuckling and reaching for her clothes. The clothes that I had been holding hostage without even realizing it, my attention being held and distracted by the way she looked standing there.

"Yeah, yeah, of course. My bad…" I said, embarrassed and slightly mortified that I had been staring at her, basically drooling over the way she looked standing in her bathroom, half naked.

"It's all good. I have the same moments with you." Ivy said, winking at me and then turning around to get changed. "I'll hurry."

"So where do you want to stay if we aren't staying here?" I asked, Ivy leaning back toward the door to look at me and answer.

"I thought maybe we could get a hotel room. I don't like the idea of being here until we apprehend him. Clearly I thought this place was safe but I was wrong. Neither of us will be able to sleep at all if we feel like someone is going to break in during the middle of the night." Ivy said, adjusting her shirt and then walking into the bedroom.

"Yeah, I don't know if I am gonna sleep, regardless." I said, taking a deep breath, my nerves starting to build as the time seemed to move faster the longer the day went on.

"True, but since we didn't really sleep last night, at least if we are somewhere that he doesn't know about, we might have a chance at getting at least a nap." Ivy said, smiling at me, both of us thinking back to the night before. My stomach doing flips the more I let myself think about all of the things we had done to each other.

"You are right. And I still need that coffee anyway." I said, realizing that we had officially been up for over 24 hours apart from a small nap. "Or I won't make it to tomorrow."

"Let's go." Ivy said, grabbing the small bag she had packed and walking out of the room toward the front door.

****

"Yeah, we are safe Chief. I don't know how he got into my loft but I wasn't going to stay there and find out either. We stopped and got something to eat and now we are at a hotel." Ivy said, pressing her cheeks against her iPhone, looking back at me, her eyes lingering on my legs sprawled across the king size bed in our hotel room, her tongue tracing her bottom lip, unconsciously.

"We will be there at 8 in the morning. If anything changes, let me know. And Chief, please be safe. It isn't just Olivia he wants dead." Ivy said, breaking her stare from me and turning around, her face looking at the wall in front of her. "If you need anything, please call." Ivy said, hanging up her phone and staring at the wall.

I stood up off of the bed, walking up behind her, letting my arms wrap around her waist, holding her tight against my body. "Chief will be okay. I know you are worried but he is a strong man. I am sure he has been in much worse situations than this." I said, trying to comfort Ivy.

"Yeah, he will be okay. He always is. I just need tomorrow to get here already. Kind of over worrying about it already… I don't know what Scott's end game is and it's bothering me." Ivy said, placing her arms across mine, pulling my arms tighter against her.

"His end game is to see us all dead, it seems. But we aren't going to let that happen. Hopefully Chief has some sort of idea about how to handle tomorrow." I said, laying my head on Ivy's shoulder, the smell of her cologne infiltrating into my lungs.

"Yeah, he wants to debrief us all in the morning and come up with a plan of some sort. We don't know what we are walking into but if we can all be on the same page, that will help. We are meeting at the station around 8 so we can come up with a plan and then we are leaving before your parents get there. All of the other officers know to detain them and hold them until we get back so that they are safe." Ivy said, taking a deep breath, her chest rising and falling slowly. "We don't need them there. The more people we have there, the more dangerous this situation becomes. However, once he realizes your parents aren't coming, things could get bad."

"There is a chance someone could die tomorrow, isn't there?" I asked, regretfully, a sinking feeling in my stomach again, as it became more real, more clear to me that tomorrow could be truly the worst day of my life, the last day of my life.

Ivy turned around and looked down at me, holding my forearms, her eyes filled with concern and fear. "I don't know what's going to happen tomorrow, but I do know that I will keep you safe, regardless. I won't let anything happen to you."

"If it comes down to it, I would rather he hurt me than you or Chief. I am the one he really wants, the one he blames for everything that went wrong in his life, the one he has been chasing after this whole time." I whispered, closing my eyes, the sheer exhaustion from the last few days, hitting me like a ton of bricks. "I'm drained. Feels like we have lived a lifetime in just a matter of days."

"Yes, yes it does." Ivy said, leaning her face toward mine, her cheek brushing against mine, her fingers still lingering on my forearms, tracing my skin. "Thankfully, it's almost over." Ivy whispered.

"Hopefully…" I whispered, looking up at Ivy, moving my lips toward hers, letting them press against hers, my hands moving up to her cheeks, gripping both of them in the palms of my hands, our lips dancing with one another, my feet lifting up and onto my tip-toes, Ivy's breathing staggering slightly.

"Baby, we don't have to do this…" Ivy said, breathless, in-between kisses, "I know you are exhausted emotionally and physically…"

"Shhh…" I whispered, kissing Ivy more passionately, letting my lips envelope hers, my tongue tasting her lips, my hands sliding through her hair, tugging lightly. "I need you…."

Ivy pulled my shirt up and over my body, my hair bunching up and then falling back onto my shoulders. My hand swiping my hair and pushing it over to one side, finding her lips again as quick as I could. "I want you…." I whispered, tugging on the belt of her pants, letting the latch clang as it came loose, the noise instantly making me more turned on.

"I want you too… I just…." Ivy whispered, my lips pressing against hers again, making her quiet, my tongue flicking across her lips, her tongue teasing forward, dancing with mine. "I just want to make sure you really want this right now…There is so much going on, I get it if you don't want to…" Ivy said, breaking away from my kiss.

I stopped for a moment to look up at her, the hair in her pony tail slightly disheveled, her cheeks slightly pink and glowing. The look of concern on her face for me, melting my heart. I had never been with anyone who thought of me first, who wanted to make sure I was okay, wanted to protect me and make sure they weren't taking advantage of me.

"Ivy... I... want you. I need this, I need you. That's what I need right now..." I whispered, letting my fingers drop to the top of her pants, un-buttoning her jeans, my fingers pulling the top of her zipper down, her boxers becoming exposed. "I feel things with you that I have never felt with anyone else in my life... You make me feel like the outside world doesn't matter anymore... You make it all go away for a little while."

"Come here..." Ivy said, lifting my body up and off of the floor, wrapping my legs around her waist, her muscles bulging as she held me against her body, my face leaning down to kiss her again, my lungs begging for air, my teeth dragging against her bottom lip, sucking and making little moans escape from the base of her throat.

Ivy carried me across the room to the chair in the back corner, sitting me down and then dropping to her knees, her face inches from my body, my stomach quivering as her fingers drug across the top of my breasts and then down to my abdomen. "Put your hands on the arm of the chair and spread your legs..." Ivy demanded, biting her bottom lip, her eyes looking at me with thirst, desire and need.

"Or what?" I asked, smirking and winking at her, waiting, purposefully not following her instructions.

"Or, I have handcuffs in my bag that I can go get." Ivy said, her lustful eyes refusing to leave mine.

"Officer Ivy, you wouldn't dare handcuff me to this chair, would you? I said, biting down on my bottom lip and leaning forward toward her, my lips searching for hers.

"Nu uh, that's breaking the rules. I didn't say you could move." Ivy whispered, pressing her hand gently against my chest, pushing me back into the chair. "Arms on the chair, legs open… Now." Ivy urged.

"Yes ma'am. Whatever you say Officer…" I said, moving my hands to the arms of the chair. My fingers spreading, letting my nails dig into the fabric, my hips shifting in the chair, spreading and opening, making room for Ivy. "You can have or do whatever you want."

CHAPTER 19

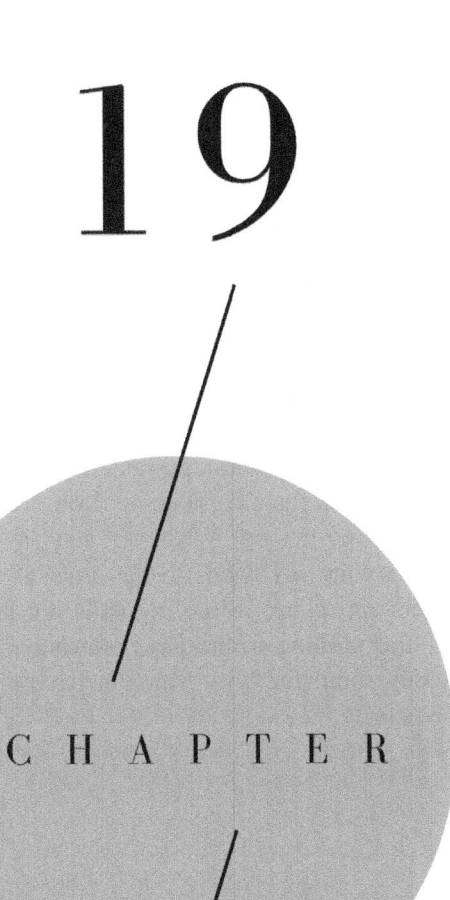

"Are you ready?" I asked, nervously fidgeting with the seam of my pants, pulling at the loose string, trying to distract myself.

"Yeah, it's almost 8, Chief is probably already in there. More than likely he has been here for a while." Ivy said, looking over at Chief's squad car parked a few rows over. "Chief has always said, 10 minutes early is late."

"Shit, if I get somewhere 10 minutes late, I am doing big things with my life." I said, chuckling and pulling on the door handle to Ivy's car, swinging the door open, the cool air sliding across my skin, leaving goosebumps behind. "Ready or not." I whispered, placing my feet on the gravel outside of the car, pushing myself out.

"It's going to be okay." Ivy said as she stepped out, her boots kicking the gravel in front of her as she walked toward the other side where I was standing.

"It just doesn't feel like that right now." I said, turning and walking past her, hopping up and onto the sidewalk in front of the police station, looking at the bushes in front of the front windows, admiring all of the colors that the leaves had turned.

I opened the front door, waiting on Ivy to walk through, her body exchanging places with me, holding the door for me, "I don't think so." She said, smiling at me.

"Well, thank you." I said, walking into the front reception area, everyone looking up at me. Their facial expressions immediately changed, a look of stress crossing all of their faces.

"Follow me. Chief's probably in his office…" Ivy said, walking past the main desk and around the corner to the hallway we had been in yesterday with a row of offices lined next to each other.

"Chief?" Ivy said, knocking on the outside of his door.

"Come in." We both heard at the same time. Ivy opened the door and walked in, chief sitting at his desk, a look of worry streaming across his cheeks.

"Have a seat." Chief said, pointing at the chairs in front of him.

"Everything okay?" Ivy said, realizing that Chief was being a little off, that there was something on his mind, something he wasn't saying out loud.

"Yeah, just wanting to make sure we do this the right way. We have no idea what we are walking into today. He made it clear he doesn't want us bringing back up but I think I am going to have a squad car that hangs out down the road at the abandoned gas station. It's still a few miles down the road but then they can get there quickly if we need them." Chief said, sitting back in his chair, pulling his glasses from his nose and rubbing his eyes.

"Chief, did you go home last night?" Ivy asked, her eyes making contact with the pillow and blanket on the couch beside us.

"No, I stayed here. I had some files I needed to review and I knew I needed to be here early anyway. This is a big case. Biggest we have ever had." Chief said, putting his glasses back on the bridge of his nose, grabbing the cup of coffee that still had steam dripping from it, tossing half of it back, a deep groan escaping his lips. "When we get there, I will go in first. Ivy you follow and Olivia, you can either stay here or you can go, but if you go, you will stay with Ivy the whole time."

"I'm going. It's me he wants. If I don't go, everyone could end up dead." I said, picking at the loose string in my pants again, my eyes refusing to look at either Chief or Ivy. "Any way I can get a gun?"

"We can't do that…" Chief said, regretfully. "You aren't an officer and I can't just hand you a gun. But Ivy does have a taser in her desk that you can use, it's her personal taser, not officer issued. I don't want you going in there with nothing but we can't let you take a gun with you, I'm sorry."

"No, I get it. I would probably shoot the son of a bitch anyway the second I saw him. The taser will work." I said, watching Ivy stand up.

"I'll get the taser and then I think we should probably get ready to go. We will be a little early but it's way out there and I don't want Olivia's parents getting here before we leave. The other officers know not to tell them where he wants us to meet him, right?" Ivy said, looking back at Chief.

"Yeah, I have told them to be quiet about it all. No one is going to say anything. They are going to have them wait in your office and if they try to leave they will make sure they can't." Chief said, standing up, adjusting his belt and walking around the desk, his hand reaching for Ivy's shoulder. "We are a good team, it will all work out. Just follow my lead and no matter what, protect Olivia and yourself."

"I have no intentions of leaving anyone behind, at all. We will all be just fine." Ivy said, "Come on Olivia, we will get that taser and then we can go."

As the words left Ivy's mouth I stood up, following behind her, looking at Chief one last time. He looked scared, he looked nervous. But above all of that, he had a look on his face of concern for Ivy. Ivy was his daughter, she was his everything and I knew that no matter what happened, he would make sure she was safe, that she was taken care of. Chief would die before something happened to his little girl.

"Chief is being weird." Ivy said as she walked into her office. She flipped the light on and walked around to the side of her desk, pulling on one of the drawers. "Can't put my finger on it but I don't like it, regardless."

"I think he is just worried about you, you are his daughter and my brother is a raging psychopath. He is unstable and he is a hard read. He has had erratic behavior this entire time. I'm sure Chief just doesn't want anything to happen to you." I said, lingering in the door way, waiting on Ivy.

Ivy dug around in her desk, finally finding the taser she was looking for, pulling it out and whispering, "Ahh."

"Yeah I guess that's what it is." Ivy whispered, shutting the drawer to her desk and walking back around to the doorway where I was standing. "He just isn't ever like this. I have seen him on some terrible cases and I have never seen him acting this way."

"Did those cases involve you at all?" I asked, making eye contact with her, her eyes starting to water slightly.

"No, they didn't." She whispered as she walked out of the door, reaching her hand back for me to follow her.

We walked back through the lobby meeting Chief at the front door of the station, our eyes all meeting before we walked through the doors. It was in this moment that I knew there was no turning back, that as soon as we walked through those doors, our lives would never be the same, regardless of what happened or what didn't happen today.

"I say we take two squad cars. If he is going to believe Olivia's parents are with us, we have to have enough room that they could ride with us." Chief said as we walked back into the parking lot.

"Yeah, I agree." Ivy said, looking off across the parking lot, zoning out for a moment.

"I told the guys to follow behind us. They should be getting their things ready as we speak and following shortly." Chief said, starting to veer away from us toward his car, "See you both there. Just follow me, I've been to this place more times than I ever wanted to."

Ivy and I walked to her car, opening the doors and stopping to look at each other for a moment over the top of the car. "Just breathe." Ivy whispered.

"I'm trying." I said, looking back at her. "Chief will be okay."

"We all will be." Ivy said, ducking and putting herself into the car, my body lingering for a moment, taking in one last breath of fresh air, every negative emotion from the last few days threatening to explode from my chest at any moment.

I opened my car door and slid into the front seat, mentally trying to prepare myself for what was about to come, the anticipation creating more and more nervous energy. I could feel my legs starting to shake, each muscle in my body twitching in angst knowing that within the next hour we would be standing directly in front of the man who had been trying to ruin my life.

I just couldn't believe that, that man was my brother. The person that I had spent half of my life looking for, the man that I thought I looked up to and was concerned for. How could it be that the big brother, the guy who used to read me stories at night time and tell me not to be anything like him was the man creating all of these horrific nightmares in my life?

"You gonna put your seatbelt on…? Chief is waiting on us…" Ivy said, looking across the squad car at me, my mind jolting back to reality.

"Sorry, I just had a moment…" I said, reaching for my seatbelt, pulling it close to my body and letting it snap into its receiver. Ivy almost instantly threw the car in reverse to back up, Chief pulling onto the street in front of us, our car following closely behind him.

"No, that's okay. I just don't want to be late. This place is quite a drive out there and I have only been once." Ivy said, her eyes fixed on Chief's car in front of us and the road.

"What's it like?" I said, looking out of the window, watching as all of the people walked down the sidewalk, smiles on their faces, their life completely normal, unlike ours.

"It's… not a good place. Well, it wasn't a good place while it was open." Ivy said, slowing down to stop behind Chief at a red light. "Everyone said it was better to end up there than to end up at Juvy, but I would disagree. I had a friend that went there and they came back, different. Not like your brother, but just not themselves. I don't really know what they did there or what the boys were forced to do, but I know that my friend said that he would never go back. He would never send his kids there, that it was absolutely atrocious. He suffered PTSD from it for quite some time, if he even ever overcame it."

"Oh…" I muttered, turning my vision to the front window of the car, the lights on the back of Chief's squad car shining back at us. "Do you think that's why my brother is like this now?"

"I have no idea. Maybe?" Ivy said, shrugging her shoulders and pressing on the gas. "He hasn't exactly tried to tell us why he is feeling what he is feeling… besides the shit he has been doing. I do know that it was so bad when the state came in, the stuff they found was so terrible, they were shut down almost immediately. The state wiped every trace of their belonging to it away like it never existed. That's why you can't find any information on it when you try to look it up. They made it disappear."

"Jesus… I don't know that I even want to know why it was shut down. I guess, well it's just that, it's my brother. None of this is okay, none of this can be taken back, my best friend, she can't be brought back to life. Those other girls, they can't either… I just wish I knew why. I want and need to know why…" I said, pressing my jaw into the palm of my hand, laying my head against the passenger side window.

"I want to know why too… So many lives, ruined, for what? Even if the boys home was horrible to him, I don't understand how killing all of these people, fixes anything…" Ivy said, the car falling silent as we both sat there knowing we didn't have the answer, that neither one of us could fathom why any of this was happening or why my brother could have committed such terrible acts.

The majority of the rest of the ride we sat in silence, the shadows from the trees and the road shining and flickering into the car window. It was broad daylight but the trees hung so high above the road, towering and leaning over the top of each other that, you could barely see anything. The sun shut out from the rest of the world. The roads were winding, twisting and turning, desolate the further we drove.

"It's like another world out here…" I said, breaking the silence, the frightening atmosphere around us, making everything a little more stressful. "I haven't seen a car for at least the last 10 miles." I said, realizing that we were alone, in the middle of nowhere. Ivy, Chief and I, the only souls still driving on this road.

"Yeah, once you get to this point, the only thing out here for the most part is an abandoned gas station and the boys home. It isn't a dead end but most of

Oregon avoids this area. Good things don't usually happen out here, especially when its dark. Thank God he wanted to do this during the morning and not at night...." Ivy said, her eyes following the back of chiefs car, her fingers glued to the steering wheel, her knuckles starting to turn bright white. "I still haven't figured out why he wants us here during the day though, seems odd, to me that he didn't want to do this at night."

"Yeah, I had the same thought. He has done everything he can to scare the ever loving shit out of us, why make us come up here in the daylight. I just can't believe I haven't ever come out this way. My parent's always told me to avoid it, but I didn't really know why. They made it sound like it was just a dangerous highway and I had no reason to come this direction..." I said, looking over at Ivy, realizing that they didn't want me to know the boys home existed, that they didn't want me coming this way for more reasons than it just being creepy and dangerous.

"He probably knows it doesn't matter if it's day or night, the further out here we go, the less likely anyone can hear us or know we are even out here." Ivy said, the words nearly knocking the breath out of my chest. I had been trying to avoid thinking about any of this too much, trying to act like we weren't heading straight toward the scariest man I had ever come in contact with. But every time Ivy said a little bit more, I realized, there was much more in her thoughts than she was sharing with me.

"Once we get around this corner, I think we are there." Ivy said, pointing at the curve up ahead, the abandoned gas station on our left across the road. The gas station looked like it had been closed for years, the sign hanging down, lopsided and barely attached. The windows had been shot out and there was graffiti down the side of the building that read, "Stop now, while you can." I felt a cold chill go down the back of my spine, my nerves building and steadily piling on top of one another.

"There it is." Ivy said, pointing to the old boys home sign that was hanging on a metal fence along the property line. The paint was so old that it was starting to flake off, the words barely legible anymore.

"Fuck…." I whispered, taking a deep breath and gulping back my distress. I could feel my stomach starting to twist in circles, the pit of my stomach starting to flip and flop so hard that I thought I was going to vomit.

"This place is creepy as hell." I whispered, the trees hanging over the top of our car, the road seeming darker than it should for broad daylight. The bumpy dirt road slamming against our tires at every move.

"It was creepy the last time I was here, but this time, puts that to shame… This isn't exactly what it used to look like…" Ivy said, looking over at the overgrown foliage that was starting to come onto the dirt road. The barbed wire fence starting to rust from the years of rain and weathering. My memories instantly shot back to the first night, the night when Scott started chasing me, his body towering over mine, a barbed wire tattoo exposed on his arm.

"Oh my god…" I whispered under my breath to myself, Ivy overhearing me.

"What Olivia?" Ivy said, concern crossing her face.

"He had a barbed wire tattoo, remember?" I said, my eyes fixated on the fencing that lined the entire property.

"Yeah, I do now." Ivy whispered. "Makes sense now."

I looked up, finally breaking my stares away from the fencing, Chief's car coming to a stop at the main building of the boy's home, his break lights shining into the front of the car, my breathing coming to an absolute stand still.

"I feel like I could throw up." I mumbled.

"Just breathe. No matter what you do, don't forget to breathe. Follow mine and Chief's lead and if I say leave, I need you to run. I need you to run back to the car like you haven't ever ran before. Here…" Ivy said, extending her hand toward me, her keys laying in her palm.

"I'm not leaving you Ivy." I said, refusing to take the keys.

"Olivia, take the damn keys." Ivy said, laying them in my lap, her voice stern. "This isn't a time to act like a bougie badass. This man is unpredictable. We have no idea what we are walking into right now. Take the keys, put them in your pocket and if I say leave, you leave. Got it?"

"Whatever." I said, grabbing the keys and throwing them into my pocket. *I am not going anywhere without you. No way.* I thought to myself, finally gathering the courage to open my door, my feet sinking into the wet muddy ground. Ivy got out on her side at the same time Chief stepped out of his squad car, his hand instantly moving to his gun. We all came together, walking towards the front of the home that had seen better days.

The front of the building had a wooden stair case leading to the front of the house, the wood planks starting to fall apart, crumbling right in front of our eyes. The bushes and vines were starting to grow over the front of the house, the front door standing open, cracked. The wind blowing so hard it was almost howling, semi screaming at us.

You could tell the house had been white in its past life from the chipping paint that was holding on by a thread. The last little bits threatening to fall off at any moment, the old exposed and rotting wood left behind, uncovered and starting to deteriorate. The windows were beat to hell, cracks and holes spattered all across them from the years of vandalism and destruction that had occurred.

There was a sign still hanging on the front of the house that read, 'Memories will come & Memories will go, but our Presence will never leave you.'

"Olivia, I see it." Ivy said, looking over at me, the expression on my face unshakeable, her hands on her gun, pressed so tightly her hands were starting to turn a light shade of red.

"That's where that came from." I said, looking over at her, Chief staring at both of us with a bewildered look on his face.

"The notes Chief, look at the sign above us." Ivy whispered, his eyes reading the words, his face changing as he realized what we had both already noticed.

"Come on." Chief said, carefully walking up the broken wooden steps, trying to avoid falling through the front deck. Ivy and I both followed, my body as close to Ivy's as I could possibly get, my hand on the taser gun inside of my hoodie pocket. *This damn taser might not keep me from dying, but it's the only thing I have*, I thought, letting my fingers slide over it, tracing it; holding onto it for dear life.

Chief reached the door that was cracked and propped open. He pushed it open, his gun still ready to fire at any moment. The room was dark, almost pitch black from the plywood covering the inside of the windows, the squeaking and squealing of the front door, like nails on a chalk board, echoing in and out of the room. The sound of the trees whipping back and forth behind us, teasing us, making the room feel that much more horrific.

"Hello?" Chief said, his foot steps making the boards of the floor moan with each step, a banging noise coming from the back corner of the room. Chief pulled out his flashlight and placed it beside his gun, pointing it across the room, looking from one side to the other until he spotted something; his flashlight stopping almost instantly.

"Mrs. White? Mr. White?" Chief shouted, my eyes darting to the corner of the room that he was pointing his flashlight, their bodies laying on the floor,. Drips of blood leading from the front door to where they were both laying.

"Nice of you to join us. Just on time." A woman's voice uttered, her body hidden.

"That's the voice… Ivy, I think I know where I have heard it before…" I whispered to Ivy, her face looking at mine. Our bodies still close to the front door, Chief standing in front of us. My mind flashing back to the first night at the bar. "I think she was at the bar. I don't know why I just remembered that."

"I know that voice, too..." Ivy said, her thoughts starting to spin, her eyes scanning the floor, trying to remember where she knew it from.

"That's right Officer Ivy, think as hard as you can. You and Olivia both know who I am. Surprised with all those years of police training you haven't figured it out yet... And Olivia, well I doubt she is capable of figuring anything out on her own." The voice echoed, still hiding from us, a sinister laugh piercing every exposed beam above us.

"Why don't you just come out, show us who you are!" I screamed, starting to lose my cool, fear driving my ego, making me feel like I could conquer just about anything or anyone.

"Oh but that would be so easy. Wouldn't it? I was right in front of your face and you couldn't even sense it. Ivy on the other hand, didn't seem to care for me, but I thought that was because she was too interested in you, instead of doing her job..." The woman's voice said as it reverberated, my mind lost. I was trying so desperately to scramble and figure out what she was talking about.

"Maybe, I should just go get your medicine again, since you like to be a whiney bitch?!" The voice shouted, my brother's evil laugh following, lingering in the air. *It's that fucking nurse. The nurse from the hospital, she is how he knew I was there. But what the hell does she have to do with my brother?*

I thought, my eyes darting over at Ivy. "It's the nurse, Michelle." I mouthed, her head shaking as we both started piecing things together.

"What do you want from us? From me?" I said, taking a step forward, closer to Chief.

A man's voice spoke up, a familiar voice, "I want to see you suffer like I had to suffer. I want you to feel what I had to feel all those years that I was shipped off, sent to rot. I want you to feel what Sophie had to feel after she left me to die. What Sophie had to feel right before I murdered her." Scott said, his voice ringing in my ear drum like a knife piercing my soul. "Where is mom and dad, *SIS?*" His voice spat, his anger starting to build, the words leaving his mouth starting to get shakier and more unstable. *Why did he just say sis like that?* I thought, barely processing what was happening.

"They are outside. I told them to stay in the car. No reason for them to be in here, this is about me and you." I said, taking the lead, standing side by side with Chief, Ivy stepping up to where we were, her shoulder brushing mine. Chief raised his flashlight, Scott's silhouette finally visible in the light of the flashlight.

"Are the White's still alive?" I asked, trying to visualize their bodies, trying to see if they were still breathing.

"For now…" Scott said, sadistically.

249

"Got a nice little 'special' cocktail like you did… Amazing what happens when you mix a little Vicodin, Valium and blood pressure meds together." Michelle chimed in, her laugh catching me off guard.

"Honestly, I should have just killed them too. I knew you couldn't stay away if I said something about MY parents! Why would you? Always trying to be the golden girl, always trying to do whatever you can to get the glory, huh? Keep riding on those coat tails honey, clearly it's gotten you far in life." Scott screamed.

"What do you mean, YOUR parents, they are my parents too!" I shouted, Scott taking a step further into the light, his face starting to become more visible, his hands on a gun, pointed straight at me.

"Oh, you think so, huh?" Scott said, laughing in the most horrific tone, the sound of his laugh matching the banging in the back corner, my eyes starting to twitch with each loud thud.

"Guess they didn't share everything with you like I thought they did…" Scott said, "Why should that surprise me! This whole family is made up of liars, made up of THIEVES! Everyone trying to create the perfect glasshouse full of BULLSHIT!" Scott roared.

"Wanna know a funny story, *SIS?!*" Scott yelled, his voice starting to crack again. "They aren't actually your parents. They adopted you. You are just as much trash as I am. Someone else's wasted goods, tossed away like you didn't even matter. See funny thing is, my life was perfect before you came along. I was their golden boy until the new baby came into the picture and then it was like I didn't even matter, like I was just last weeks TRASH!" Scott shrieked.

"I could never do anything right, I was always a failure in their eyes, can't let poor little miss Olivia see anyone do anything wrong ever. In fact, did you know that's why they sent me here?" Scott screamed, his hands pointing all around the room, his spit flying through the air as the words were leaving his mouth.

"No, Scott, I didn't know that. I had no idea they even sent you here. I was at summer camp and when I came back home you were gone, it was like you never existed. Mom and dad told me that you had moved out and didn't so much as leave a note…." I said, trying to get him to calm down, hoping that the more I talked to him he would cool off and settle his emotions. I knew the more angry he became, the more hostile he would be and the more of a loose cannon he would become.

"Oh, right, you expect me to believe that! Ha. Ha. Ha." Scott said, in a menacing tone. "Mom and dad sent me here to be beaten with metal barbed wire. They sent me to be forced to eat dog slop and starve to death. I was treated like human garbage Olivia and you want me to believe that you thought I would just move out at 16 and never come back? REALLY? Maybe you are dumber than I thought!"

"Scott.... I really didn't know. I had no idea. Mom and dad didn't tell me any of this." I said, thinking back to when I came home from camp, looking in his room, realizing that his stuff had been packed up and his room was cold and empty. "I was worried about you. I even spent the last few years trying to find you, looking everywhere, but I never could find a trace of you." I said, hoping that Scott would eventually listen to me, that he would take even a second to be rationale with me.

"Olivia, you really think that I am going to believe you? Your best friend, the person you always hung out with, even after I left, was SOPHIE! The girl who left me to die in the woods, the girl who didn't care about anyone but herself, she didn't ever tell you? It's not like she didn't know what happened to me, like THEY, didn't know what happened to me!" Scott shouted, pointing toward the White's, his foot making immediate contact with Mr. White's face, blood splattering across the floor, Mr. White's groans barely audible. The light from Chief's flashlight flashing across the floor, pointing their direction, blood dripping from their faces. They had bruises covering their cheeks and neck. He had been beating them for god knows how long. Torturing them, their hands tied together with zip ties.

"Scott, you need to stop. Sophie never told me any of this, I had no idea you were here, or that Sophie had done that to you or that our parents weren't my biological parents.... I loved you Scott, I looked up to you, I knew you were better than all of this. I didn't mean to get you in trouble, I was just trying to protect you. I knew you were better than the alcohol and drugs." I said, throwing my hands around the room.

"Well, you might have, but mom and did sure didn't. I want them in here, now!" Scott demanded as Ivy stepped forward.

"You can have them when you hand over the White's, alive. That was the deal, remember?" Ivy said, her voice booming, confidence radiating from her skin.

"Oh, you think you are going to barter with ME?!" Scott said, chuckling, the horrific sound of his laughter carrying through the empty abandoned room, tree branches banging against the glass outside of the house, my body jumping every time another noise popped up out of nowhere.

"I said, I want mom and dad in this room and I meant it. I get them and you get the White's!" Scott screamed, Michelle grabbing his arm and pulling on it.

"Scott, this is getting out of hand!" Michelle screamed, trying to get him to settle down.

"Get the hell off of me you stupid bitch, you are only here because I needed you to get to them!" Scott shrieked, shoving Michelle to the floor. Her body hit the rotting wood, cracking it and falling through to the underneath of the house.

I jumped, the shear force of his shove and her body breaking the boards apart like they were nothing, shocking me to my core. Caused me to almost jump out of my skin. I had been holding my breath, scared to breath, scared to make a wrong move. I wasn't prepared for him to make such a violent move.

"I said, get me my parents and I meant it! You have about 30 seconds to bring them in here before I blow every one of you away! Especially... Chief and Ivy! You two are who brought me here, dropped me off and left me. You both abandoned me even though you knew this place was hell. You knew what they would do to me! You had seen what they did to other boys that were brought here and you did nothing to stop it!" Scott yelled, his body starting to shake, his hands waving his gun around erratically, his anger building with each word he spat.

"Scott, we didn't know how bad this place was. We fought to get you here instead of Juvy. We thought it was the better option, that it would be less of a punishment. We didn't know what this place really was until after it was shut down." Ivy said, taking a step closer to Scott.

"Don't you dare come any closer. Don't you dare try to tell me that you didn't know either. I think it's pretty fresh you all expect me to believe you had no clue what was going on, that you are all innocent in this...." Scott said, starting to wave his gun around, tapping it to the side of his head. Banging it across his face. "This. Place. Made. Me. CRAZY!" Scott said, slamming the end of his gun against his temple, sweat starting to drip from his face, the veins in his forehead bulging, his cheeks turning bright red as his spit shot across the floor.

"Scott, your parents aren't here." Ivy said, gripping the trigger of her gun tighter, ready to shoot at any moment. Preparing herself for what was about to come once Scott registered that we hadn't played his game how he wanted us to.

"WHAT!" Scott said, enraged. His gun pointed right at my head, ready to shoot.

"I told you, to play the game, or you would REGRET it!" Scott said, his jaw tensing up as he uttered the words. "Guess you don't really care about my *sister* like I thought! Just needed someone to take advantage of. Someone to FUCK." Scott screamed, his finger reaching for the trigger of his gun, pulling back at the same time Michelle's hand popped up from under the house, grabbing his ankle and pulling him down. His gun went off mid air, piercing the ceiling of the house, pieces of wood splintering off and splattering across the floor.

Scotts body flung across the floor, the gun flying the opposite direction as it struck the ground beside him. Michelle stood up, blood running down the side of her face, a look of psychotic rage enflaming in her eyes.

"I gave up everything for you Scott! I am the only reason you got out of this god forsaken hell hole in the first place! Everyone else was going to leave you to rot but I loved you... I told you we shouldn't be doing this. I tried to warn you!" Michelle screamed, starting to sob angry tears, her arms waving and flinging as her voice escalated, her jaw line becoming more defined as she grit her teeth together.

"You stupid B..." Before Scott could finish his sentence, Ivy stepped forward, pointing her gun at Scott's face, his hand out of reach from his gun.

"If you move another inch, I will blow your brains out. Don't believe me, try me. This is my game now." Ivy said, kicking his gun across the room, her gun still pointed between his eyes, his body laying on the floor, his breathing staggered.

Ivy bent down, pulling her handcuffs form her belt and slapping them across his arms, pulling him up to his feet. Chief ran behind her grabbing Michelle and pulling her up from underneath the house. He hoisted her onto the wooden floors, putting handcuffs on both of her wrists as well, her face covered in tears and blood from the fall.

I ran over to the corner, dropping to my knees, checking on Mr. and Mrs. White, both of which had been beaten and battered, their breathing extremely shallow. Their clothing was covered in blood splatters and dirt.

"Oh my god, I am so sorry…" I whispered, knowing they wouldn't hear a word I was saying, their bodies barely hanging on. "I'm gonna get you help, as fast as I can." I said, standing up and turning toward the front door of the house, watching as Ivy and Chief pushed both Scott's and Michelle's heads down and shoved them into the back of the same police car. Ivy and Chief shut the doors to the back of Chief's squad car, locking Scott and Michelle in and ran back up to the house.

"They need help, fast." I said, pointing to the White's. "Neither one of them are breathing very much and they both look like they are knocking on deaths door." I said, my breathing staggered, the adrenaline rush from the last hour starting to dwindle down, reality starting to slap me in the face.

Chief grabbed his walkie and pressed the side button, shouting into his hand set for back up asap. Screaming that we needed medical help. My legs started to shake as I realized that my nightmare was finally over, that my brother was finally caught and locked in the back of a cop car. I felt my legs starting to buckle as I was standing in the middle of this abandoned room, my whole world starting to crash down around me. I felt a relief sweeping over my body at the same time. Ivy reached over and grabbed me, keeping me from falling to the floor, holding me as I wept in her arms, my emotions overcoming me.

"It's going to be okay... We got him." Ivy whispered, holding me against her chest, her lips pressing against my hair, kissing the side of my head. "He is going away for a long time, maybe even forever." Ivy said, her voice reassuring me that he couldn't hurt me or my friends or family anymore.

"Thank God" I said, as Ivy started guiding me out of the boys home, holding me down the stairs so I wouldn't fall, chief following behind as an ambulance pulled up the house. The lights from the ambulance were flashing, bouncing off of the trees, little bursts of sunshine peeking from behind the leaves.

# CHAPTER 20

You ready?" Ivy whispered, walking up behind me as I was standing in our bathroom, her arms wrapping around my waist. She let her chin rest on my shoulder, her eyes meeting mine in the mirror.

"Yeah, almost... I just need to put on some mascara and then I am ready. Well, as ready as I will ever be, I guess..." I said, looking back down at the sink, grabbing my mascara bottle and tinkering with the lid, Ivy's lips kissing the side of my exposed shoulder, close to the strap on my dress.

"No rush, Court doesn't start until 9, we still have about an hour before we have to be there." Ivy said, her lips trailing up to my neck, lightly kissing my skin. I took a deep breath, enjoying her lips on my neck, wishing that we could just stay here instead of dealing with my brother, again.

"I know this is important, for every one. But I don't ever want to see his face again. I'm only going because of the White's, Sophie and all of those other girls... If it wasn't for them, I wouldn't be stepping foot in that room. I don't even want to see my parents, I'm honestly dreading it. I still haven't spoken to them since that day." I said, opening the mascara bottle and applying it to my eye lashes, my mouth opening slightly.

"I wouldn't be going either. I am going because all of those people and because of you." Ivy said, her hands gripping tighter to my waist. "Those people are important too but it's time you get to see justice served. It's time for you to feel like that door can finally be closed. I want to see the day that you can breathe fully, that you can live the beautiful life you were meant to have."

I finished putting on my mascara and stopped to look at Ivy in the mirror, her eyes compassionately looking at me. I turned my body towards her, leaning up against the floating vanity, pulling her closer to me. "But what if justice isn't served, people have done similar stuff to what my brother did and they didn't get what should have been coming… What if they let him off with an easy sentence…" I said, the words stinging as they left my lips.

"That won't happen." Ivy said, her fingers reaching for my chin as I looked down at the floor, her fingers pushing my face up, forcing me to make eye contact with her. "He killed multiple people and attempted to kill more. They have all of the evidence that they need to put him away. Both him and Michelle are going away for a very long time, Olivia."

"You are right, I am just stressing out. This has to be one of the scariest days of my life." I whispered, Ivy's hands pushing my chin back up again, her lips pressing gently against mine, her body pulling me in for a hug.

"I know and I get it. But it will all work out. He will go down for what he has done and then we can move forward. You can relax and unwind." Ivy said, kissing me on the cheek and then turning toward the door. "I'll be in the kitchen when you are done." Ivy said, turning to walk away.

"I'm ready. As ready as I will ever be." I said, grabbing my clutch purse and walking through our bedroom, into the hallway, following Ivy.

The rest of the car ride to the court house was basically silent. My thoughts were racing in every direction possible. My mind wandering into different places, envisioning what could happen depending on what the judge decided Scott's punishment should be. I couldn't speak. I wasn't even sure what I should say anymore.

We pulled into the parking lot of the court house. My parents car was parked at the front of the building. They were standing outside of the car, waiting to hear what their son's punishment would be, the clouds above lingering in front of the sun and then moving, light beaming across the green grass of the court house lawn.

Ivy parked in a parking spot down from my parents, next to the White's. Ivy put her car in park and took a deep breath, her shoulders relaxing a little now that we were here. She took her seatbelt off and turned her body to mine, her hand resting on the gear shift in the middle of the car.

I stopped, letting my finger run across her ring finger, tracing the small wrinkles in her skin, thinking about how badly I wanted to ask her to marry me. Thinking about how much I wanted to really start my life with her, but now wasn't the time. I wanted it to be perfect, I wanted it to be special and meaningful. I needed this day to finally be over so we could take steps in that direction.

Ivy was the first person I had ever stopped long enough to think about a future with, she was the only person who had ever made my world stand still. Even with how we met, even with how horrific the last few months had been, she was the calm to my storm, she was the peace to my suffering.

At first, I was worried that we had connected because of the trauma we were both experiencing. I was scared that once we found the killer, we would fizzle out just as fast as we had come together, but it was quite the opposite. Now that my brother was apprehended, it felt like our lives were meant to collide, that we were destined to find one another.

"Just remember, no matter what happens in that courthouse today, we will all get through it, together." Ivy said, moving her hand above mine, squeezing it gently, her cheeks forming a reassuring smile.

"You are right. Regardless of what happens to Scott and Michelle today, they will both be put away and we can try and go back to some sort of normalcy.

Sophie and those other girls spirit's can finally be at peace, hopefully." I said, taking my seat belt off and opening my door, letting the sun hit my knees. The warmth reassuring that everything was going to work out.

"Let's go." I said, standing up, pulling the base of my dress down to my knees, nervously pressing the wrinkles flat. Ivy walked around the car and shut my door behind me, letting her hand rest on the base of my back.

"Is this okay?" Ivy said, her arm wrapping closer to my body, my hip grazing the belt of her dress pants. "Your parents are looking and I didn't want to make you uncomfortable."

"I really don't care what they think anymore. They have lied to me for my entire life, created this demon, trying to hide from the truth. I refuse to be like them, I refuse to hide my truth, to present a glasshouse for anyone." I said, confidently pulling Ivy closer to me. "We are together. Chief knows and is happy for us, your mom knows and is thrilled. If they can't be happy for me, happy that I found someone special, then they can piss off. The perfect daughter they wanted just might not exist. I won't put on a show just because my mom wants me to, I will be who I want to be. And I will be with who I want to be with."

"I just wanted to make sure. Your feelings and desires mean everything to me." Ivy whispered, leaning down to kiss the side of my head, her nose lingering and grazing across my hair. "I never want to make you uncomfortable or not think of your feelings." Ivy said, guiding me toward the front door of the courthouse.

My steps feeling both daunting and powerful at the same time. Every click of my heal against the pavement getting louder as I realized that this was my chance to slam the door to hell closed. I let go of Ivy's waist and found her hand, letting my fingers slide between hers, locking tight, my fingertips pressing against the back of her hand, squeezing.

"Olivia, Ivy…" My dad said as we approached the end of their car, his head nodding as he acknowledged us both. My mom was standing up against the bumper of their white Land Rover, a look of disappoint and disgust on her cheeks. She couldn't bare to acknowledge me, or us.

"Dad." I said, nodding at him, squeezing Ivy's hand a little harder as I made eye contact with my mom, blatantly ignoring her back. *If she can't acknowledge me or Ivy, other than disgust, then she can reap what she sows.* I thought, smiling at her as I walked past her, leaving her and my dad to walk in behind us.

"Do you think things will ever go back to the way they were?" Ivy asked as we found a seat near the back of the court room.

"I have no idea. Mom is the one who has a problem with me being gay, she has always had a problem with everything, to be honest. Before things with Scott, I looked past it. I thought it was my fault because I had the DUI. I thought that because I lost the glorious career she wanted me to have it all fell on my shoulders, but that's not fair. People make mistakes, clearly she has had her fair share as well, but she can't see that. All she can see is herself, her image. Maybe if she worried about loving her kids and her family more, instead of what everyone else thought of her, life would be different." I said, shifting my weight from one hip to another. Pulling on my dress again, pushing it closer to my knees, placing one knee over the other. "Besides, she knew I was gay before you, she refused to believe it, refused to listen to me. I hadn't ever had a real serious relationship before you so she didn't have to worry. You changed that and she is mad. Not my fault. I didn't ever lie to her or hide who I was."

"...But now that everything has come out about Scott, I refuse to take the blame for how my parent's feel. I refuse to let her always control me. Scott is to blame for his decisions, he did these awful things, not my mom. However, mom throwing him away like he was trash, didn't help and she is trying to do it to me now too. I have no doubt in my mind that the reason my mom and dad were fighting way back when is because my dad didn't want to punish Scott the way my mom did, he is a kind man. He isn't perfect, but he tries. And now that mom knows I am with you, she doesn't support it and thinks stonewalling me emotionally will get me to change my mind. She tried to do the same thing to my dad when she was not so secretly sleeping with other men. He didn't agree with her, so she blocked him out. It's what she does."

"Ivy, I don't want you to ruin your relationship with your parents over me, that isn't fair and it's not something I could ever ask you to do…" Ivy whispered, her dress shoe tapping on the floor anxiously.

"Guess it's a good thing you didn't ask me to do it then. And besides, it isn't just about you. You aren't the one who hid that I was adopted my entire life. You aren't the one who told me my brother ran away and then covered up their tracks. You had nothing to do with any of that." I said, letting my hand slide across her thigh, my fingers squeezing toward the middle of her muscle. "I think we are getting started." I said, looking up at the front of the room as the judge walked in from her office door.

My eyes instantly shot over to the side Scott and Michelle were going to be sitting in, waiting for them to come into the room. Everyone's voices getting quieter as the judge started shuffling folders across her desk, looking through the information in front of her, the jury lining the right side of the wall. Each one of the jurors looked anxious about this case; their body language was radiating throughout the room with each foot tap, finger nail chew and nervous shift.

"There they are." I said, watching as Scott and Michelle were being ushered into the room. They had handcuffs on their arms and legs both, their steps more of shuffles. It was the first time I had really been able to see Scott since the bar. The night we saw him at the boys home the room had been so dark that I couldn't make out much of his face, similar to the night in the woods when he was standing over me. Ivy and Chief had escorted them out of the house so fast and I had been worried about the White's. I didn't even have time to get a great view of him. It felt like I was seeing him for the first time in my life.

"I can't believe I didn't recognize him." I said, still in disbelief that I hadn't been able to put the puzzle pieces together sooner, feeling a bit disappointed in myself.

"You hadn't seen him in years. I can tell you that I saw him in the hospital and he looks nothing like he did back then. He has changed, a lot. The drugs and alcohol haven't done him any favors either. He looks old, very old." Ivy said, reassuring me. "I wouldn't have recognized him if I saw him either."

"But he is my brother, I should have known." I said, whispering, as the room grew near silent.

"All rise." The judge boomed, her voice carrying across the room. I stood up, looking throughout the droves of people, searching for my parents and the White's.

My parents had found a seat toward the front, on the opposite side of Scott and Michelle, facing where they could see Scott's face. The White's had found a spot near the back, like Ivy and I, lingering. Neither one of them looked like they wanted to be here, dark circles forming under their eyes and most of their skin color pale white. It looked like they had spent most of their days since Sophie's passing, sobbing.

"Everyone can have a seat." The judge shouted, my legs starting to feel like jello again, my nerves starting to creep back up as the hearing was beginning, the first few minutes of the everything was bleeding together, my ears tuning everything out.

"Michelle, to the stand please." The persecuting attorney spoke, turning their body toward Michelle, watching her as she stood up and scuttled toward the stand. She sat down, shifting her body in the chair, chewing on the inside of her lip as she took oath.

"Michelle Williams, that is your legal name, correct?" The attorney asked, standing beside their desk, resting one of their hands on the desk.

"Yes, that is correct." Michelle said, leaning into the microphone in front of her, her voice cracking as the words left her mouth. Her voice didn't have the same confidence that it had, had before, when she was the one toying with our lives.

"All right Ms. Williams, can you tell the court how you know Mr. Scott Sanchez?" The attorney asked, moving in front of the desk toward the stand.

"I met him in junior high. We were the same age. He was a good friend of mine." Michelle said, looking down at her lap, refusing to make eye contact with the attorney.

"And how did you two come to know each other as adults?" The attorney asked again, wanting more clarification. "Please be as detailed as possible."

"I was at the same party Scott was at the night he had his wreck. When the cops showed up I went looking for him but never could find him. I ended up leaving with someone else, I had no other choice. I had to get out of the party or I was going down…" Michelle said, her mind lingering back to old memories.

"I went to Scott's house to check on him the next day but neither him or his parents were there. I called a few of our friends to see if they knew where he was and no one could tell me anything other than he left with Sophie and a group of younger girls that were at the party. I didn't know Sophie personally but I knew of her, it's Carlton, not like you don't know everyone on every corner… I ended up going to her house and asked her what happened. She looked like she had seen a ghost but wouldn't talk to me. She tried to slam the door in my face but I grabbed the door and stopped her. I begged for her to tell me what was going on, and that's when Mr. White came to the door..." Michelle said, looking back down at her lap. "Mr. White told me that I needed to leave and that I needed to stop putting my nose where it didn't belong. I knew something was wrong so I kept asking around, prying and pushing for answers. Scott was not only my best friend but I had a crush on him, I wanted to make sure he was okay." Michelle said, looking toward the back of the room in the White's direction.

"And what happened then?" The attorney said as Michelle stopped talking and changed her attention over toward Scott, their eyes locking to one another, Michelle's face full of regret.

"I finally got one of the girls to tell me what had happened. It took me a while but they finally caved. By the time I had some answers Scott was long gone. I stopped by Scott and Olivia's house and his mom came onto the porch screaming for me to leave that Scott was gone and she didn't know if he would ever be coming back... She said she hoped the place she had sent him would change him and if it didn't he could just stay the hell away like I could." Michelle said, my eyes darting over to Scott, who was shifting in his seat back and forth, the back of his head twisting side to side, popping his neck.

"Anyway, I figured out that she had sent him to the boys home so I made a plan to try and get him out. I went to see him every week. We would stand by the barbed wire fence at the property line and come up with ways to get him out for good. But there were always so many eyes watching that it took me a while. Eventually I helped him escape and let him stay at my parents lake cabin they never stayed at. I helped hide him there until we both came up with a plan to rectify what had happened. I never intended for anyone to get hurt, I just wanted to get even. I wanted everyone to know what they had stolen from us both. It started out as more of a harmless revenge pact than what it turned into…" Michelle said, tears starting to form in her eyes.

"I know this may be hard to believe but none of this was ever my goal. At first Scott and I talked about small pranks, ways to get even, more basic things like slashing tires, messing with peoples houses, things like that. But eventually Scott started escalating, wanting more, getting more angry…"

"Scott started working for the 'rich' people apartment complex as a maintenance guy, hiding in the shadows of his past, under a fake name. He didn't want anyone to know he was still here, that he hadn't run away. He spent day in and day out lifting weights, trying to find ways to not look like his old self…

I was in nursing school, trying to figure out how to make enough money so that we could just leave, escape it all, forget what had happened to us and to change our lives. Scott on the other hand just kept coming up with more and more plans. The reason he started working at the apartment complex is because he knew that Ivy had moved in there. He knew she was someone he was going to go after, and he had to be smart if his plan was going to work... I didn't know that at first. I thought he was just saving money so we could run off together." Michelle said, making eye contact with Scott again, the tears starting to stream down her face uncontrollably.

"If you need a minute, you can have it. There are tissues beside you also." The attorney said, walking back to their desk and sitting down on it, still facing Michelle.

Ivy grabbed my hand and held it tightly, shifting her body closer to mine. The warmth from her body comforting me as I was starting to get emotional. I had never heard any of this before. It was like I was meeting my brother for the first time all over again, hearing his past was stirring up every feeling possible.

"I thought I had finally convinced him to run away with me and to leave everything else behind, to forget about getting even...I thought that since I had graduated nursing school and gotten a job at the hospital that I could save some money and we could eventually leave but then he texted me saying that he had seen Olivia at the bar. He asked if I would please come be with him, that seeing her again was igniting something inside of him. Something he felt like he couldn't control and it went downhill from there... The longer the night went on the more he drank. The more he drank, the more his rage started growing. I tried to get him to leave, to go home, but he kept staring at Olivia, watching her every move. Eventually he started watching Sophie too, stalking the both of them. I had no idea that he had already murdered those other girls. I never put the pieces together. I feel so stupid, I should have known. I should have known that he was the one behind it, but I didn't want to believe it was him. I didn't want to think he could actually do something like that."

"What happened when you left the bar?" The prosecutor asked, my eyes darting over at the jurors who were all listening intently.

"I begged him to come on that I had to work the next day, but he refused. He said he wanted to go for a walk. He had calmed down by this point, the bar was closing and he said he would find a ride home. I should have known that was a lie but he promised me that he wouldn't do anything stupid. He said that he just needed to walk off the alcohol. I ended up leaving him standing on the sidewalk and went home. I had no idea what he was going to do that night with Sophie or Olivia for that matter. I went home and fell asleep. Woke the next morning to go to work and found him passed out on the couch, covered in blood. I asked him what happened and at first he wouldn't tell me, but then he finally broke down and told me he had followed Sophie and Olivia to their homes. He said that he had chased Olivia into the woods and almost got caught. He said he then circled back around to Sophie's house and then to their parents...

At first I felt like I could vomit but then I knew that if I loved him, I had to help him. I had to find a way to fix this so we could run off together. I asked him what I could do... That's when he came up with the idea for me to see if Olivia was taken to the hospital. He begged me to add some of my valium that I was prescribed for anxiety to her list of meds so that he could come to the hospital for a little bit. I really don't know what made me do it, but I followed his wishes. I paid attention to Ivy and Olivia's conversations and I lingered in the hallway to see what they knew. I was trying to figure out if they knew who he was, how we could get Scott out of this. I even tried to ask him if we could just run off, act like things with Sophie never happened, leave Olivia alone and find somewhere to hide until things blew over, but he refused..." Michelle said, starting to hyperventilate, her tears becoming heavy sobs. Michelle looked up and across the room, scouring it for my parents, for the White's and for me. "I am so sorry. I don't know why I participated in any of this. I am so sorry... by the time I realized what I was involved with it was too late, I was in deep... I thought I loved Scott, I thought he loved me, I just wanted us to have forever, I just wanted all of the bad things that had happened to go away, I never wanted any of this to happen, I never wanted anyone to get hurt. I should have just run when I had the chance. I should have turned him in instead of participating, I am so sorry…"

Michelles words felt like knives piercing into my ears. You could hear a pin drop, everyone in the room in dead silence as reality was hitting them.

"That is all for now, your honor." The attorney said, turning around and sitting down at his desk. Ivy turned to look at me, tears streaming down my face. So many women dead for nothing, for absolutely nothing… Ivy reached her arm around my shoulders, pulling me in closer, holding me tight against her chest.

It felt relieving to understand, to know how the puzzle pieces fit together, to be able to paint a picture of what had happened but it also hurt, it burned like a raging fire deep in my chest. It felt like someone was squeezing the breath out of my chest, lighting fire to my soul. My best friend had been murdered for vengeance for something that she had done when she was just a pre-teen. Those other girls, just the same… There was no reason for this callous type of hate, this cold horror.

"I hope this is over soon." I finally muttered in between tears. Ivy's body holding me close, her lips pressing against the side of my head again.

"Me too. Me too…" Ivy whispered, leaning back against the pew we were sitting in. The trial continued on, footage from the hospital being shown to everyone in the room. Even footage from Scott at Ivy's apartment complex, sneaking into her apartment.

Each attorney asked Scott and Michelle both a series of questions, answers unfolding before our eyes, my mind blown by their responses. Scott felt so cold. His responses were heartless, like he had no shame, no guilt in the world for his decisions. The women he had killed meant nothing to him, they were disposable. I was ashamed that he was even my brother, that we were related at all, in any way, even if it wasn't by blood like I had thought.

CHAPTER 21

"The jury has found a verdict. All rise." The judge said, my stomach starting to quiver, my insides feeling like they were being turned to mush. The last few hours had been brutal. Hearing brutal details from Scott, hearing things I never wanted to hear anyone say out loud, much less my "brother". I hadn't cried this much in my life.

I was in shock. Complete and utter shock that someone could sit on the stand and talk about these women like they didn't mean anything, like their lives were meaningless. Like they were trash. He was one of the most stone cold and satanic men I had ever met. His words feeling like the knife he had tried to slice my arm off with.

My parents were sitting in the front, sobbing and tucking their heads, hiding from the world. My mom clearly refusing to acknowledge that they had any part in any of this. I could see it on her face. I could feel it in her energy. She felt like they had done everything they could. She refused to acknowledge that they had thrown him away just the same as he had thrown those girls away. He might not have been murdered physically, but his emotional needs were abandoned. He was casted away like he was a disgrace. He was just a teenager, making stupid decisions. He needed someone to love him, to show him that they cared.

"Scott, you are first. The jury has found you guilty on all counts of pre-meditated murder in the first degree. You are being sentenced to life in prison with no parol. Michelle, the jury has also found you guilty of being an accomplice in the murders, as well as attempted murder of Olivia in the hospital and the White's... You are being sentenced with life in prison with no chance of parol. You both should be ashamed of yourselves. Michelle, it makes me sick that you would have ever called yourself a nurse. You took an oath to protect and do no harm, clearly that was all for show." The judge said, her gavel hitting the tray on her desk, her words crisp and clear.

    I felt every emotion I had been trying to shove down into my chest over the last few months come spewing out. My tears turned into rivers across my cheeks, my knees collapsing out from underneath me, my body slamming against the pew with relief.

    "Olivia, YES..." Ivy said, relief overcoming her body, her energy relaxing as the words continued to settle into our minds.

    "He is gone. For good..." I said, looking up at the ceiling, pointing "Sophie, now you can relax. You can have your peace." I whispered, my sobs coming out in droves.

    Ivy wrapped her arms around me, hugging me close to her body, her chest caving around mine. "We can finally breathe..."

    I looked up, still crying, scanning the room for the White's. Their faces were filled with relief and satisfaction. This was never going to bring back their daughter. It was never going to give them their baby girl back but it was the closest they were ever going to get to justice, to winning for their daughter.

"Sophie can rest now." I whispered, smiling and grabbing Ivy closer. I held her as tight as I could, solace overtaking my entire body. The rest of the room cheering as Michelle and Scott were drug back out of the court room and back into the pits of their new personal hell.

"Can we please go now?" I asked, looking at Ivy, wanting to get out of that room as fast as I could, the walls starting to feel like they were closing in. "I need some air. Today has been a lot. In a good way, but a lot…"

"Yes, let's go. We did what we needed to do." Ivy said, grabbing my hand and leading me out of the court house into the court yard, the sun hitting our faces, warming our skin. Birds were chirping across the way in the grassy area, bouncing from one tree limb to another. The air felt thinner, easier to breathe, like a weight had been lifted from my shoulders. The lump in my throat that had been residing there, starting to slowly dissipate.

"This is the first time in months I don't feel like I have to look over my shoulder anymore." I said walking toward Ivy's car, stopping in front of Ivy's passenger door.

"I get it. I feel the same, honestly." Ivy said, resting against the front end of the car. "Even though this is a job I do daily, nothing has ever phased me to the level that this case has."

"I just can't believe that's how he got into your apartment. It makes sense now though. I never could figure out how he could get into your apartment without a key card, but that's because he didn't... When they showed the security footage of him walking into your apartment hiding in his old maintenance uniform with his hat tucked hiding his face, I almost lost it." I said, thinking back to the night when we walked up to Ivy's open apartment door with the note taped to it.

"Yeah, when they showed that I stopped breathing for a moment. I thought that apartment was bulletproof, clearly I was wrong. I never thought about an old employee, like Scott, being an issue. It never even crossed my mind." Ivy said, looking down at the concrete, her foot tracing the painted line on the ground, focusing hard.

"And I still can't believe Michelle was standing outside of my room like that in the hospital. How did no one notice her doing that? I feel like someone had to have thought that was strange? I guess not though..." I said, thinking back to the hospital and how Michelle had walked in right at the time I said I needed my nurse. Realizing that she had probably been standing there for a while, creeping on us both.

"Well, I guess, none of that matters now. What matters is that this nightmare is finally over, they are both going away, and we can finally breathe…" I said, looking into the courtyard, watching the birds play back and forth, realizing that one of them was a mourning dove, imagining that they were Sophie and the other girls. Hoping that they finally had peace now that Scott and Michelle were being put away.

"Thank God." Ivy said, turning her body toward mine, pulling me toward her, her hands sliding around my dress to my back, holding me. "It's about time for you and I to be able to live our lives without fear. I will say…" Ivy whispered, tucking her neck and face toward my cheek, letting her lips press gently against my skin, "I'm thankful that through all of this, I at least had one good thing come out of it. You."

I pulled back, a serious look crossing my face, my eyes meeting Ivy's, "I love you." I whispered, the words slipping from my lips like honey, melting off of my tongue. My heart started to pump harder as I realized what I had just said to Ivy, that it was the first time I had ever told her I loved her.

Ivy looked me dead in the eyes, holding her stare, her beautiful hazel eyes shining brighter as the sun bounced off of them, making them sparkle. She moved her hands from my back, grabbing my hands and holding them in both of hers, lifting them to her lips, pressing her lips softly against the backs of my hands. "I love you Olivia, with all of my heart." She whispered, kissing my hands again before pulling me into a warm embracing hug.

"I could stand here for hours just being held by you." I said, whispering in Ivy's ear, kissing her cheek and then her shoulder, breathing in her intoxicating cologne. "I am forever thankful for you."

"Olivia!" A familiar male voice echoed across the parking lot.

I looked up to see Mr. White running toward me from the front court yard of the court house.

"Mr. White! Hey, I'm sorry I didn't stop to talk to you. I had to get out of there." I said, feeling slightly embarrassed. I had been avoiding him and his wife since the boys home. Avoiding the PTSD I felt every time I saw their faces, trying to hide from a conversation that I knew had to eventually happen. Sophie was a special girl, someone that I cared deeply for, she was a soul that I would never feel whole without, someone that had been there for me through my darkest times.

It felt surreal, to have to live life day to day without her, to have to remind myself that I wouldn't see her name cross my phone anymore or that I wouldn't be able to call her anytime something exciting happened in my life. It felt unreal that I wouldn't hear her obnoxious wheezy laugh ever again. I knew that my therapist would tell me I needed to find a way to cope, that staying in the denial stage wasn't healthy, but it had felt like the easiest thing to do. It was the quickest way to move forward with life.

"No, No. Don't feel bad. I felt the same way." Mr. White said, slightly breathless from running across the parking lot, his suit slightly disheveled, his tie pulled loose. "I have something I wanted to give you. I know Sophie was your best friend and I think she would want you to have it."

"Oh... Okay." I said, slightly caught off guard, emotions starting to stir in my heart again.

"Here." Mr. White said, pulling out a necklace I had given Sophie when we were little. Tears instantly surfaced in my eyes, threatening to stream down my face, my breath ripping from my chest.

"It's the Mourning Dove necklace you got her. She never took it off, ever. Even when she was an adult. I think she would want you to have it, it was special for both of you." Mr. White said, his lips starting to quiver as he spoke the words, "She loved you very much. We have heard more stories about you than you can ever imagine. Please don't ever forget how much she cared for you." Mr. White said, handing the necklace to me, his eyes welling with tears as he turned on his feet toward his car. "Maybe we can get together soon." He said, walking toward Mrs. White who was already waiting at their car.

I nodded, letting the tears flow, looking at the necklace in my hand, tracing the beautiful grey and tan colors of the necklace. Letting my fingers trace each intricate line that had been carved into the stainless steel.

"Of course." I said, looking back at the White's as they got in their car, a small smile emerging from the tears trailing down my cheeks.

"I gave this to Sophie when we were about 10 years old, I think. It was somewhere in there. I had no idea she still wore it." I said, still looking at the necklace, holding it tightly in my hands. "I gave it to her because her grandmother passed away. She said she didn't know what she was going to do without her grandma, that she felt lost. The mourning dove is supposed to symbolize that your loved one is watching over you…" I said, instantly looking up at the trees across the way, the dove still sitting on one of the lower hanging limbs, looking right back at me.

"She clearly really loved you, Olivia. It meant something to her and now it can mean something for you. She is watching over you, I truly believe that." Ivy said, gripping her hands over mine, the necklace still in my hands.

I kept looking at the bird, watching it's movements, listening to it chirping. *I don't know if I am just being emotional or if that's really Sophie, but either way, this feels like it has to be a sign, it has to be*

Sophie's way of telling me she is here with me. It has to. I thought to myself, pulling the necklace from my hands, Ivy's hands dropping to her sides.

"Can you help me put it on?" I asked, turning around and handing the necklace to Ivy.

"Yes, of course..." Ivy said, grabbing it and placing it on my chest, my hands lifting my hair up and off of my shoulders, Ivy's fingers pressing the clasp shut.

I turned around, looking back at the tree limb, searching for the dove that had just been sitting there, but it was gone.

"Let's go home." Ivy said, opening my car door for me. My eyes still searching the trees, hoping to see the dove one last time. *This isn't goodbye forever, I will see you again and it will be just as magical as the day I first met you. I love you, Sophie Woafie. Don't hate me, I know you hated that nickname, but it will always be your special name in my heart, reminding me of your laugh, of the friendship we had. You were and always will be my best friend. No one can ever fill the space you had in my heart, I will wear this with pride and know that you are always here, that you are always protecting and looking over me.* I thought to myself. Finally letting myself smile through the tears, sitting down in the seat of Ivy's car, the door shutting, Ivy's face becoming clear through the window. Ivy stood there, holding her hands together in the shape of a heart, a giant smile on her face.

God, I'm so in love. I could stare at her smile forever and it still wouldn't be enough time.

A second dedication is in order for my college best friend. Without her in my life I might not be here. I promise I will eventually get that otter tattoo, the one you never had a chance to get. It's on my bucket list. I will make sure it happens, just as you wanted. I will forever miss you. Forever miss your friendship. This isn't goodbye, this is see you later. I love you best friend.

Printed in Great Britain
by Amazon